WHERE THE HEART LIES

Don R. Kabrich

Published 2018 by WC Publishing
Printed in the United States of America

For information, contact:

WC Publishing
4625 Cedar Ford Blvd.
Hastings, FL 32145

WC Publishing
an On-Target Words company

DEDICATION AND ACKNOWLEDGEMENTS

This book is dedicated to Kevin Morehead and Paul Mardis. Two of the bravest men I ever knew. This work would not have been possible without the support and assistance of my family, editors and publisher.

I want to thank Nancy Quatrano, Danielle Jordan, David Crossman, Paul Avalone, and, of course, my wife Karen, my son Conner, and daughter Sydney.

Letter to My Readers,

Although this book may appear to be an ordinary action novel, it is not. It is an extra-ordinary story.

The pieces all come together in the end and I believe it will be completely satisfying. There are a few "aha" moments that I wish for you. This book is unique in that it is a screenplay, wrapped in a novel.

It begins as if you are a Hollywood executive reading, page by page, a movie screenplay. After the screenplay, the executive is greatly affected by the story. The book then moves to our main character, Cory, who wrote the screenplay, reflecting on some real-life experiences in life and war – until such time as we see Cory *living* his life, not *writing* it.

To help you keep this straight, the screenplay-specific font type is always used for the screenplay, so you'll know what part of the story you are reading.

This novel is about being brave enough to risk our hearts in order to care about others, even when we have been hurt too many times. This book is a journey that a young man goes on to find out where his heart truly lies. We are all on that journey to some extent – or have experienced it.

This story is also about heroes and the sacrificial-type love it takes to be one. We all have moments where we have reflected this type of selfless love in our lives. We often don't consider those moments noble perhaps, but they are. The father in this story is hurtful, selfish, and disappointing, but as you will discover, he is also a hero who just wants his son to live a good life after all.

And finally, this book is about a divine destiny. It is a screenplay written at a time in the young man's life that closely resembles the real life that takes place in the story. What is amazing is how the two stories first met to become this novel. The prologue of this book is about an old man in a Victorian house. You will need to remember it when you come to the end, as the story comes full circle back to that moment.

There are flashbacks, flash forwards, and everything in between. In the end, the name of the character of this book, and in the screenplay, is a character named Cory whose life was both marred and made beautiful by a place called Iraq which, when read backwards, as in the reflection of a mirror, reads, "qarI" which is pronounced, "Cory".

I hope you enjoy this journey and that it positively impacts your life. The writing of it was definitely a blessing to me.

Don R. Kabrich

PROLOGUE

INSIDE AN OLD VICTORIAN HOME - DARK AND
QUIET. MAN IS UNIDENTIFIABLE, OLD AGED.

With every shade drawn, most of the mid-
morning sun is kept out. Old furniture and
appliances fill the home. A grandfather
clock stands tall and ominous, clicking
slowly and rhythmically next to a steep
staircase. Although the long-necked hammer
never stops rocking, the hands ceased to
move long ago; symbolic of a home, a time
and place that never moves forward.

Down a darkened hallway in a small room,
a slow-turning fan slaps its edges
harmlessly against a wind-carried drapery
panel. Beyond the room, at the end of the

hallway is a much larger room. A faded
Persian rug covers the floor, and a large
dark leather chair occupies its center.
Seen from behind, thick clouds of whirling
smoke gently rise to the ceiling. Beyond
the chair is an old film showing on the
plaster wall. A gray projector clicks
loudly as it rotates the reels. The film
slacks and catches every other turn. Dust
particles dance in the light.

In the chair, sits the elderly man
consumed by what he sees. Almost bald
except for some white lengthy strands of
hair, his bony hand slowly repositions the
smoldering pipe in his mouth.

As he stares at the film through his
thick horned-rim glasses, he sits proudly.
Honorably. Military ceremonial music
blares from the projector's speaker. In
black and white, the film runs orderly
clips of military duty.

The film displays whole battalions
marching crisply in pass and review
parades. The viewer sees barracks life
where soldiers and their quarters are

being inspected. The soldiers are sharp and disciplined as they stand at attention. They move quickly when ordered to. The rooms are spotless, and every piece of brass and tile shines brightly.

The film moves to another scene. Soldiers are down on their hands and knees scrubbing the floors and windows, all focused on their tasks.

Again, the film moves on. This time, the viewer is taken to combat training. Men leap and roll, shoot and throw grenades. They move like machines and act like the soldiers they seek to epitomize.

He is captive in his own memories, recalling the days when his military life shone brightly. He recalls the discipline, the professionalism, the duty, the honor, and he smiles. But he is happy for only an instant. He cannot relive what he misses so much. He is immensely proud to have served; he's proud of little else in his life.

FADE TO BLACK

CHAPTER ONE

At eight o'clock pm the sprinklers move back and forth watering the lush Beverly Hills lawn. Inside the modern contemporary all glass estate house, a Hollywood executive sits behind his desk. Wearing a blue polo shirt and black slacks he also wears frameless, stylish glasses.

In his mid-forties, his brown hair is neatly trimmed and parted off to the side giving him the appearance of a throwback to the late 1950's. He swings his feet up on the desk, leans back in his leather chair and opens a large brown envelope.

The light blue, 8 ½ by 11-inch card stock paper encasing the pages is the standard hole-punched format for a screenplay, with the necessary two brass-colored fasteners; one at the top and one in the bottom. Flipping it open, he scans to the middle of the first page. He pauses a moment to think about the title, "Where the Heart Lies."

Like he's done a thousand times before, he turns the page and the story begins.

* * *

FADE IN:

(DARK DESERT NIGHT - HEAVY AUTOMATIC GUNFIRE AND EXPLOSIONS A DARK FIGURE IS BEING QUICKLY CARRIED BY HIS ARMS AND LEGS TO THE AWAITING HELICOPTER.)

The heavily wounded man who has been blown up can only see the dark faces of those who hold him while running. They yell at each other to motivate one another to survive and counter attack. They fire their weapons.

The wounded soldier is not part of the action and feels as though he is just watching the action above him. As the sound of his own breathing and laboring heart beats take over, the Black Hawk helicopter doors open, and the door gunner continues to suppress the quickly approaching enemy with heavy automatic fire. He motions to the soldiers to hurry.

The wounded man looks up beyond the shadowy faces and helmets who struggle to carry him. He searches the night sky and sees the stars between the parting clouds above.

FADE TO BLACK

* * *

The executive rests the script in his lap. *Good cinematic possibilities*. He rubs his eyes, sips a cup of coffee, then reads again.

After a solitary moment of quiet darkness, another scene opens, and the executive knows he's found where the story really begins.

The Van Halen rock song noted on the script gives the era away. The scene opens with an explosion of sights and sounds and the exec smiles. This is what a good script does. It transports the viewer to another world. He drops his feet to the floor, takes another sip of cold coffee and leans back to enjoy the journey.

ARMY BARRACKS - DAY

Rock music blares out of tiny speakers and the Army barracks shake and vibrate. Young soldiers of every race, half-dressed in boots and green fatigue pants, jokingly push and shove each other. Several guys with their tee-shirts off, they are stuffed into their back pockets and dangle halfway out.

Another soldier swaggers through with a hat barely hanging on the back of his head. He carries a worn-out mop over his shoulder that leaks dirty water onto the faded tile floor. He enters the latrine, and instantly plugs his nose. With a swiveling motion, he rotates the mop off his shoulder directly down and into a toilet. He dunks it around a little. Satisfied that the mop is ready to go, he drops the lid down on it. As he withdraws the dark, grungy mop head, he twists it and presses the lid down to ring it out.

Men half-heartedly buff this and clean that. They check their watches counting the minutes until they can stop. Some of them pass the time by blowing soap bubbles. Others make little hand puppets out of their cleaning rags.

A soldier comes running out of his room holding his hand over his mouth. His cheeks swell with the vomit that barely makes it to the sink, the familiar stench of German beer and Jägermeister boiling up in the stomachs of Army privates every Monday morning. Hardly anyone notices as the kid stumbles back to his room.

A paper airplane goes whizzing by the guy's head whose mop, once again, hangs comfortably over his shoulder dripping foul water to the floor.

"Just another attempt to sabotage my secret mission," he says in fun. "Sarge must be crazy if he thinks I'm gonna mop the commander's office again!"

"Yeah, yeah," one of the soldiers says, "you've been shaming all week anyway, Jones. It's only right you get the job."

One of the paper airplane aviators sends another plane down the length of the corridor.

Jones looks at him with phony contempt. "Yeah? You want me to mop your room up with this when I'm finished?"

Everyone laughs.

FIRST SERGEANT'S OFFICE - DAY

CORPORAL MCGUIRE stands at ease. The First Sergeant could win a look-alike contest for an aging Barnie Fife from the Andy Griffith Show. He sits, looking thin and tired, wearing military issued horned-rimmed glasses. His protruding Adam's apple moves up and down with each swallow. His wrinkled uniform pales in comparison to the Corporal's.

FIRST SERGEANT

"McGuire, I got your orders here, but for the life of me I can't understand why you want to do this thing." (He pulls the orders closer to his face to make out the fine print.)

McGuire stands pressed and starched from head to toe. His boots glisten brightly from the fresh spit shine he gave them the night before. Standing about six feet, one hundred eighty-five pounds, his athletic figure compliments the wear and appearance of his uniform.

The First Sergeant peeks over the top of the orders and gives McGuire a look.

(Scanning him from top to bottom, he shakes his head.)

FIRST SERGEANT

"McGuire, you've been at this transportation unit for fifteen months, and in that short time, you've won five inspections, two Soldier of the Month boards, and too many three-day passes."

(Reminiscing, he raises his voice, holding his arms outstretched.)

FIRST SERGEANT

"I personally brought the Command Sergeant Major to each room for his inspection. You know what kind of disarray he found this place in, right? But, no, not you. We go waltzing into your room, and the CSM almost has a heart attack!" (His arms now gesture wildly, as he continues.)

"The floor buffed, drawers staggered with socks and shirts rolled. In the wall locker, each hanger hung two inches apart with pressed uniforms. The bed was so tight, he couldn't even pinch the spread between his fingers."

(Finally, the First Sergeant looks at him tiredly.) "Did you have to spit shine the drawer handles?" (Appearing serious for a moment, he then laughs.)

"You're something else, McGuire. The next thing I know, you're his personal driver. As if that's not bad enough, three months later, I get a phone call requesting that you be transferred down the street to European Headquarters, no less. I mean, the Command Sergeant Major in charge of *all* American forces wants you to be his driver. You kill me!"

(Cory forces a slight smile as if not very amused by all this.)

"So, you take the job, rub shoulders with the big shots, drive around only God knows where. Everybody from full bird colonel down is asking you questions. I got to tell you in the twenty-plus years I've been in this man's Army, I've never seen a spit shine go so far."

(He stands up and scratches his head for a moment. He puts his hands down on the desk with his arms locked and looks at the orders on top of the stack of papers.)

"I don't get it. It seems like you got a pretty good thing going here. Why do you want to leave?"

(McGuire clears his throat determined to get his point across.)

MCGUIRE

"I want to move on from here. I didn't join the Army to just do this. I joined up to be a different kind of soldier. I know the US Army is a disciplined, professional and patriotic place to serve, but I need to see more of it, Top."

(The First Sergeant examines McGuire's face and gives a warm grin.)

FIRST SERGEANT

"I don't know if this," (he points down at the orders) "is the right place to look, either." (Then he shrugs.) "But give it a shot if you want to."

Putting his hands on his hips, the First Sergeant says, "Ok! Listen up! The effective date of these orders is today. You have been reassigned to Special Forces Training Group, Fort Bragg, North Carolina for Special Forces training. En route, you will be required to successfully complete Airborne Paratrooper School at Fort Benning, Georgia. Upon completion, you will participate in S.F.A.S., Special Forces Assessment and Selection phase, at Fort Bragg for an additional three weeks. Should you be selected for Green Beret training, you will be assigned to the Training Group, also at Fort Bragg where you will undergo 210 days of Special Forces training."

The First Sergeant looks across the desk and meets McGuire's gaze. "Do you understand what I've just read to you?"

MCGUIRE

"Yes, First Sergeant," McGuire snaps.

FIRST SERGEANT

"Good! Now pack your bags and get out of my company!"

(McGuire comes to attention and then moves quickly to the door. As the First Sergeant takes his place at the desk, he sounds off at McGuire.)

FIRST SERGEANT

"Soldier?"

MCGUIRE

"Yes, First Sergeant?"

(The First Sergeant pauses, then slowly breaks a smile.)

FIRST SERGEANT

"Good luck."

(McGuire smiles, and gives a nod.)

MCGUIRE

"Thanks, Top."

CHAPTER TWO

TRANSPORT PLANE HEIDELBERG, GERMANY - NIGHT

McGuire is leaving the 302ND Transportation Company in Heidelberg, Germany without many regrets. He is leaving behind the kind of Army he didn't know existed.

Others had come looking for the same kind of soldiering he did: more disciplined, motivated, and patriotic. But after a time, their spit shines dulled, and their uniforms lost their starch. They'd fallen prey to the seduction of the "new" Army.

The pressure to be just like everyone else was tremendous. McGuire was different though. His desire to be outstanding was not a superficial one. Instead, it burned deep within him.

Maybe he was just intrigued by the stories
his father told him, he didn't really know.
Nothing was quite clear to him, except the
need to find a different kind of soldiering.
One where he fit in.

Becoming a Green Beret might be a bigger
bite than he should take. The First Sergeant
seemed aware of this. The Special Forces
school had more than a massive attrition rate.
Many soldiers were weeded out long before they
ever reached Green Beret training. Either
their written test scores were not high enough
or they were found to score below the physical
standards required.

Since he is on his way there, he has
obviously passed several stringent
requirements. More weeding out will take place
and he's aware of that. The Special Forces
wants only the best, and he likes that idea.
He's willing to do whatever it takes to be
included in that category. But he has a long
road ahead of him. He wonders if he has what
it takes. He isn't sure, but he's willing to
find out.

Having out-processed his unit, Cory is flying back to the States. He completes a long flight from Frankfurt, Germany and makes a transfer at J.F.K. International before landing in Detroit, Michigan. The 727 floats onto the runway with the usual skidding of tires.

In his Dress Class-A uniform, he walks through the terminals sticking out like a sore thumb. His uniform hangs honorably and he knows it.

He finds his way to the baggage claim and recovers his duffel bag. As he walks to the main entrance, people talk and stare. Some point. He doesn't pay any attention. He knows he doesn't quite fit in. He's too proud of his uniform not to wear it, though. Besides, it's regulations. He called his father prior to leaving. He said he was going to be there to pick him up.

Standing amongst the multitudes of people scurrying about stuffing bags in trunks, backseats, or wherever they could fit their belongings, he keeps a lookout for his father. Time goes on, and he checks his watch a few more times. He thinks he sees him a couple of times.

But the men he thinks resemble his father kiss and hug other waiting travelers. Cabs come and go. Shuttle buses honk at people crossing. Bag checkers stand around laughing, smoking, and eyeing the ladies.

Some kid runs past McGuire straight into the arms of a laughing, smiling dad. The man picks him up and gives the boy a big hug. After a moment, he lets the boy down. Instantly, with great excitement, the boy starts telling his father all about his trip. As only a little boy can, he tells his story. Arms waving, he stretches them out to show the exaggerated size of something. He jumps and hollers all the way to the car. His father listens intently. He pretends to hang on every word. They stuff some bags in the trunk, slam it shut, and speed off into the traffic.

Now forty minutes late, McGuire stands waiting for his father both angry and sad. This isn't the first time his father has done this to him, but he is angry with himself for expecting it to be different this time. He feels stupid standing on the sidewalk with his duffel bag. Nothing has changed, and he realizes it. Even though he's serving his country overseas for eighteen months, it doesn't seem to make a difference.

With one last look around, he makes his way back inside. Some businessman in a suit slams down a phone, and mumbles something as he passes by.

Cory picks up the receiver, deposits some change, and dials. He sticks a finger in his ear and hears the phone ring a few times.

"Whitman and Brice Incorporated," the pleasant voice says.

"Yes. May I speak to Robert McGuire please?"

"Who, may I ask, is calling?"

"This is his son, Cory McGuire."

"Oh, yes, Mr. McGuire, your father left a message for you." She hesitates a moment to find the message.

"He says he won't be available to make it tonight but wishes you to meet him tomorrow afternoon at three p.m. at the following address. It's 1330 Market Street." A long pause. "Did you get that?"

Disappointment and anger send blood rushing to his face. He pinches the bridge of his nose as if suddenly given a tremendous headache. The anger subsides, and he surrenders to the predictable circumstances. He lowers his voice.

"Yes Ma'am, I got that. Thank you." He hangs up and rests his head on the edge of the phone.

No. Nothing has changed, and he's instantly brought back to memories of his childhood. For a time, he'd forgotten about his father's behavior. But now he feels like he's ten again. Although he's hurt, his well-worn defense mechanisms quickly set in to numb him.

He walks out of the airport with his duffel bag over his shoulder. He makes his way through the greetings of family and friends reunited. He tries not to notice as he drifts off into the darkness of the big city.

Walking the downtown city streets, he spots a cheap motel. Another huge jet liner goes screaming low overhead, as it makes its final approach to the nearby airport.

Neon lights blink a portion of the word "Vacancy." Two A's and a C are burnt out. He doesn't see the word "NO," so he goes inside. Luckily, that portion of the sign wasn't burnt out, and he gets a room.

Inside, Cory lies on a swayed mattress in a white undershirt and shorts. He laces his fingers behind his head staring at the ceiling, and after an hour of watching the red neon light flash reflected on the wall, he falls asleep.

* * *

At three the next afternoon, a yellow taxi cab pulls up to 1330 Market Street, stops and Cory steps out. He's wearing a pair of dark sunglasses, a blue polo shirt, tan cotton slacks, and brown shoes.

After paying the singing, gum-smacking man behind the wheel, Cory stands alone in front of some sort of public storage facility. This part of town is ancient.

A slight breeze carries garbage tumbling along the worn, potholed streets. The railroad track sends a long train roaring by. Cory watches as each car speeds through. As the final train cars goes by, on the other side, a faded green 1989 Ford L.T.D. sits, black smoke billowing out the tailpipe. The car slowly moves, rattling and sputtering to a stop. The engine continues to spit and cough before it dies.

Stepping out of the car, a figure emerges. Robert McGuire stands before Cory in a dirty, short sleeve, button-down shirt hanging outside his pants and hair that hasn't been combed in probably a week.

He's stone-drunk and staggering awkwardly as he moves toward Cory. Mr. McGuire's been on such a drinking binge that he's almost unconscious. All of forty-eight years old, he looks sixty. His eyes are sunken and red. His hair is thin, grayed, and greasy. A thick white mustache sits under his red nose. Obviously swollen, his sick liver makes his stomach stretch the shirt buttons.

Before Cory stands a ruined man. Someone he's watched over the years, little by little, deteriorate to his present state. From as far back as he can remember Cory has watched his father slowly throw his life away. The need for alcohol subtly took over every aspect of his life. He'd changed jobs time and time again, blaming it on the job and never himself. From number one marketing manager at US Steel to used car salesman, Cory had watched him fall, helpless to change it but hoping he would. The man standing before him is pathetic and had hit bottom a long time ago. He just didn't know it.

As if nothing is out of the ordinary, Cory's father approaches him full of good cheer. Cory falls right into his role, thinking that being supportive is always best. They ignore the obvious.

"Hey, Son! Show me a salute."

Cory does his best to accommodate him with a quick salute. "Hi, Dad, you're looking good," Cory says with a hint of sarcasm.

"Stinkin' boss. He doesn't play fair, so I hit the road. You know what I mean, Son?"

"Yeah, Dad, I know what you mean." Cory puts his hands deep into his pockets and looks around. He doesn't mention last night. It wouldn't do any good. His father probably wouldn't remember anyway.

"Dad, what are we doing out here?" Cory asks, looking up at the facility's chain link fence.

His father starts to stagger forward fumbling in his pocket for a key. "I need you to help me move a few things. You've always helped me out. You always have. No matter what. You're a good kid."

"I know, Dad. We've done this too many times."

Cory's father shakes his head looking sincere. "I know. I know. Too many times. This is the last time. If I have to move again, I mean."

"You say that every time, Dad."

"You're right, Son, but it's a tough world out there. I taught you that. I raised you tough. Tried to do a pretty good job, too."

His speech starts to slur. He pauses and looks Cory over. Cory knows what's coming. Another long Army story that he's heard a million times before.

"You know. I was stationed in France. I was the most squared away soldier the Army ever saw." He stumbles.

"Everything I owned was spit-shined like glass. I was the number one soldier for five months running. I outclassed them all." He sneezes ten times in a row, and then blows out a nostril while holding the other closed. He wipes his hand on his pants.

The story goes on and on. He talks about how much he liked the Army and how looking like a number one soldier made all the difference. He got rank faster and was given a lot more responsibilities.

Cory knew first hand that those things mattered and proved it in Germany by being squared away like his father. However, now he is tired of hearing the stories.

Watching his father talk, he makes another mental note to do better than him. He's not going to end up like this. He's going to show him and everybody else that he will be five times a better soldier than Robert McGuire. His father wants to raise a tough kid, but he always thinks he's raised a wimp. He's never short of challenging Cory, especially when he's drunk. Cory needs to prove him wrong.

His thoughts circle back around, and his

father is still rambling on about one thing or another. Finally, he stops.

"Ok, Son. Let's go inside and get this stuff moved in."

He leads Cory through the gate and around a corner to an adjacent storage alley. Like garage doors stacked one by one in a row, he leads him to the one with the U-Haul in front of it. As if in slow motion, he unlocks the ten-feet-wide door and pulls it open. Various household goods are sprawled about. Most of the items won't make good yard sale items. The truck has just a few heavy items.

Piece by piece, they manage to stuff them into the small storage shed. Cory's father's complaints are non-stop, and Cory tunes them out. When they are finished, the small storage room is stuffed. As the sun begins to set, an almost eerie calm settles in the air and around Cory.

Cory hates looking at his father's condition. It hurts to see him this way. Tears start to well in his eyes. His father starts fidgeting around, rearranging things here and there as though setting up a living room.

In disbelief, he asks softly, "Dad, what are you doing?"

In a matter of fact tone of voice, his dad replies, "Help me move this table over here. Do you think this chair could go there?" He points to a small space left in the corner. "If I cleared the boxes from the sofa-"

Cory screams, "What are you doing?!"

He can't watch any more. He isn't going to let the game go on. His father is killing himself. Cory moves toward his dad and searches his eyes.

"Do you mean to tell me, that you want me to help you arrange your boxes so you can *live* in this hole? Is that what you want me to do? Is this what it's come to?" Cory pauses and tears stream down his face. "I can't do it anymore, Dad. You're killing us."

At that instant, something or someone has reached deep inside Cory's dad. Time stands still, and they find themselves staring at each other. His father's eyes also fill with tears. He begins to weep as he moves to the wall and slides down to sit on the floor. With his hands crushed against his eyes, he pours out tear upon tear. He's crying for thirty years of failure; his marriage, his career, his lost family and friends, and his life.

Cory moves to his side and sits down. He wipes his own tears while putting an arm around his father.

"Dad, it's going to be all right."

Cory's father whispers, "I'm sorry, Son."

CHAPTER THREE

747 IN THE AIR - DAY

At twenty-nine thousand feet, the plane hums smoothly along. Somewhere over Michigan, Cory stares out the window.

A flight attendant strolls by asking him if he needs anything. He doesn't respond for a moment, and then, with a half-smile, he tells her he's fine. He turns his head back to look out the window again.

He doesn't have any tears left. He thought he cried his last years ago. The few days he'd spent with his father were busy ones. After helping him find a home and giving him some money, Cory is on his way back to duty.

He finds himself thinking of his childhood and the father who raised him. He sees himself startled awake in the dead of night. He sits erect in the darkness of his childhood room, wide-eyed with terror. From downstairs, he can hear yelling, screaming, and things crashing. In his pajamas, too scared to sit still, he rips his covers off. His heart races and he moves to the hallway as his sister, just two years older than he, emerges. They freeze, and their eyes search the area at the foot of the staircase frantically. They flinch at the sound of another crash. It sounds like a riot downstairs. It's worse than usual.

In a whisper, he asks, "What should we do, Jamie?"

His sister, standing beside him in her nightgown, suddenly starts to wail and runs down the stairs.

He follows. They round the banister at the bottom of the stairs and run through the kitchen. Now inside the living room, they run toward the screams.

In a small white bathroom, the terror is

unveiled. Robert McGuire is kneeling on his wife's arms.

She's flat on her back, in a long white sleeping gown, as her husband lands blow after blow into her face. Blood sprays the walls. Each blow gets more ferocious. She kicks and screams in terror.

"Stop it, Bob! Stop it!" she cries.

Jamie screams and jumps on his back. Cory stands in the doorway frozen in fear and shock. His father turns and tries to stand with Jamie on his back.

Like a drunken bear, he stumbles and staggers, but Jamie's arms are still clutched tight around his neck.

Cory's mother struggles to her feet and aims to get past her husband who tries to grab her as she runs by.

The small bathroom echoes cries of terror and confusion. Jamie lets go of her father, pushes away and lands on her feet, then dashes after their mother. Cory is still frozen in the doorway.

As Robert stands, panting with blood smeared across his shirt, his eyes meet

Cory's and Cory sees the eyes of a demon. His fierce gaze looks right through him. This man is not his father. It must be someone else; a soulless man possessed by rage.

Robert comes after Cory and he runs, dodging his father's outstretched arms.

Robert stumbles and crashes into a planter sending it crashing to the floor beneath him. Dirt, pottery and green leaves stick to his hands as he slowly rises. His words are more like the growl of a cornered animal.

"I'm gonna kill you all! You are all dead! I'm going to—you miserable—I'm going to kill you! Do you hear me? I'm going to blow you all away!"

Cory, his mother, and sister huddle in a corner. His father bounces off bookcases and doorjambs and finally stumbles past them as he crawls up the stairs.

"Oh, my God, Mom!" Jamie screams.

Cory gets to his feet, trembling. His mother pushes the two of them quickly through the house toward the front door.

Rounding the corner at the top of the stairs, Cory's father returns. He snaps a magazine into his Colt 45 handgun.

"Go! Go! Go!" Cory's mother screams, ripping the front door open.

At three o'clock in the morning, they run down the driveway and into the street. The bullets they expect to come do not. And in the black silence of the night, in a neighborhood like any other, they run down the quiet streets.

No words are said, and the only sounds heard are that of bare feet slapping the cool asphalt. Around the corner, they hide in a large bush and crouch in the dirt like animals. They listen intensely. Far off in the distance, a few dogs bark. An occasional cricket squeaks.

Before long, Cory's head is nestled in his mother's lap. He stares up at her beautiful but bruised and bloody face. The glow from the rising sun begins to lighten the dark sky. Cory's mother starts humming as she gently rocks back and forth. He closes his tired eyes and feels her tears drop to his face. Cory feels his own roll down his cheek.

An overhead ding sounds on the aircraft and he's pulled out of his memories. The seat belt sign comes on. He shifts in the seat and sighs.

There is something about his father that he loves and hates all at once. His father needs a lot of help, but Cory realizes his father will have to help himself.

On that fateful day in the public storage shed, Cory's father found his bottom and Cory found his, too. And he discovered he couldn't handle any of it anymore.

Ever since he was a kid, he'd tried to help his father by accepting the truth about what he was and what he'd probably always be.

Apparently forgotten was the drunken terror his father placed upon them that horrible night. In not wanting to create any additional problems, the whole family just acted like it had never happened. By ignoring the events, it was as if all was forgiven and forgotten. From a very young age Cory was made to survive one day at a time.

Cory, now holding a magazine open but seeing none of it, is transported to another childhood memory. He sees himself nine or ten years old, sitting on the living room floor. It's late at night. On the other side of the room, he sees his father reclining in an easy chair. It's dark and the television casts a haunting glow. The room shows only faint shadows.

Young Cory sees the dark image of his father lying silently in his chair while the glow from a smoldering cigarette can be seen in his hand. Cory, deciding it's finally time, tip toes to the television and turns the volume down low. He sees his father suddenly move and his heart jumps.

But it's okay. His father still lies silent. Fearing the thumping of his own pounding heart might wake him, Cory slowly approaches. Heart still pounding, body trembling, he reaches and removes the smoldering cigarette from his father's hand. Burns from the ones he missed in the

past line the inside of his fingers.
Backing away, he puts the cigarette out.

He drifts into the darkness. His father
is passed out and everyone should be safe
until morning. Cory runs upstairs, crawls
into bed and tucks himself in.

From his airplane seat, Cory slams his
hand down on the food tray spilling some
juice. People from across the aisle stare
curiously as he wipes it up.

Cleaning up the spill, he swallows hard.
He's angry for allowing himself to think
freely about it. With a sigh and a deep
breath, he puts it behind him. He knows it
does no good to allow it any place.

Cory learned a long time ago that the
only one he can truly trust is himself.
He's survived so far because he knows this
kind of truth. This is what works, and no
matter how nice it would be for it to be
different, his truth is as simple as that.

He nods. The Special Forces is where he
belongs. Like him, he will find survivors:
disciplined, motivated and self-reliant.

Tapping an inside pocket, Cory pats his

orders for Airborne school. He looks out the window as if searching for Fort Benning, Georgia which is somewhere in the distance.

CHAPTER FOUR

C-130 AIRCRAFT - NIGHT

Snap. Snap.

Looking to the rear of the C-130 aircraft, the paratroopers direct their attention to the jumpmaster who is snapping his fingers. He puts his hand to his face and blows a kiss. He quickly holds up seven fingers indicating a wind speed of seven miles per hour. He then arches vigorously out the side jump door to spot-check the drop zone.

Somewhere in the middle of the pack, Cory McGuire sits entrenched in the red cargo net seats. Like sardines, the aircraft is crammed with paratroopers. They sit four rows deep, two facing in and two out. Their legs lace between the men facing them. The large green aircraft shakes, rolls, and dives like it's flying a combat mission.

Prop wash burns the eyes and skin of the half-nauseated soldiers. A red fluorescent lamp gives the dark paratrooper space an eerie glow. Steam vacuums mysteriously through the vents overhead. From the wind of the open doors at twenty-five hundred feet, and the high-pitched whine coming from the engines, a deafening roar dominates.

It's one o' clock in the morning and pitch black out. There is no moon to aid in the jump.

Cory's throat is dry as he looks around. His hands are cold and wet. He notices the eerie atmosphere that feels familiar. With approximately an extra one hundred pounds tied to them, the paratroopers sit with backs aching and straps digging into their shoulders.

Between their legs, a fifty-pound rucksack hangs anchored to their waists. A tightly stowed parachute is on their backs and a reserve shoot is strapped on their front mid-section.

A web belt, littered with canteens, ammo pouches, and butt pack hangs mounted to their waists. Green and black camouflage is painted on their faces. Tightly fastened chin straps ensure their helmets will stay on.

The atmosphere is tense as Cory watches and scans each soldier for their nervous ticks. To the right and over a few men, a small thin kid suddenly throws up into a white bag. He then stows it in his shirt. Everything brought on the aircraft must go off. That's the rule. To Cory's left, he notices another guy checking and rechecking every possible strap, clip, and snap. A couple of the other guys are acting like they're sleeping, but Cory knows better. The jumpmaster emerges again, and this time, he holds up six fingers.

Everyone on board sounds off. "Six minutes!"

The tension builds. Like a machine, the

jumpmaster follows up with the rest of the jump commands. And like a well-rehearsed play, the commands are answered.

"Get ready!" he shouts.

Everyone stomps their feet and pats each other on the back shouting, "Get ready!"

"Outboard personnel stand up!" the jumpmaster bellows. Each command is accompanied by arm gestures.

He points at the next group to stand up. The two outside rows struggle to their feet.

"Inside personnel stand up!" he screams. "Hook up!" They hook the static jump release cords to the long running cable overhead. He goes through the commands.

"Check static lines!"

"Check equipment!"

And finally, "Stand in the door!"

Everyone shuffles forward and stands tight to one another. One man from each side steps into the jump door and stares into the void. Poised and ready, they wait for the tap out. A small red light glows brightly just above the first jumper's helmet.

The jumpmaster rechecks the drop zone one more time. He sees the beacon flashing below. Suddenly, the green light comes on, and he gives the paratrooper a swift slap to his backside.

"Go! Go! Go!" he screams at them.

One by one, they file down the aisle and disappear into the darkness. Only four men back, Cory continues shuffling. He grips his static line with white knuckles. In what seems like an instant, he passes his rip cord to the jump master who is still shouting.

Cory finds the door, and suddenly he's jumping out and away from the C-130. The 150-200 mile per hour wind deafens and spins him like a great wave. Instinctively, he starts counting.

"One, one thousand! Two, one thousand!" And by two and a half, his chute rips open, jerking the wind out of him. He keeps his chin to his chest and his boots together.

With the opening shock complete, Cory is flying under a perfect canopy. He watches the shadow of the aircraft disappear into the night. He hears other chutes descending around him, but he can't see them. It's pure silence now as his chute floats in the calm breezes over Georgia. Cory pulls his quick releases, but they don't budge.

He needs to release his gear before he hits the ground. And with it hanging on a twenty-five-foot cord below him, he can know when his body will hit the ground. He struggles and struggles. He looks for the fast-approaching ground but can't see it. His heart begins racing. His eyes start playing tricks on him. He thinks the ground is going to smash into him any moment. Cory stops fighting and pulls his overhead risers to slow his decent. Suddenly, the ground brings Cory slamming in. He makes three complete end-over-end summer saults before coming to a stop.

Cory lays facing the night sky breathing hard and fast. He isn't hurt, but he pats himself down checking for injuries he might not be aware of. There are none. He hears the grunts of paratroopers dropping all around him. He can only hope none of them land on him. Still laying on the ground spread eagle, a cheerful voice walks by and says,

"How was your jump?"

Cory raises a tired arm and gives a half-hearted thumbs-up. "Real good," he drawls sarcastically.

Then beyond Cory, the trooper bellows, "Airborne!"

* * *

At 0600-hours the next morning, Cory is standing in formation.

"Where are my quitters?" is being hollered at them like a broken record.

The First Sergeant is standing in front of the formation of Airborne trainees wearing his gray Army-issue running sweats and a black baseball cap. The Airborne Cadre is affectionately called the Black Hats.

In the center of the gravel quad, Cory stands at Attention with the others. No one moves for fear of bringing unwanted attention to themselves. Eyes strain to catch a glimpse of the First Sergeant. At every formation the ritual is repeated. In the morning, afternoon, and evening, the formation of tired and beaten airborne trainees hear the call.

"I said, where are my quitters?" the First Sergeant cajoles with his hands on his hips, searching the ranks for targets.

"I've got beer and pizza waitin' for anyone that doesn't want to be here. I need quitters and I know you're out there!"

He pauses, and a deathly silence follows. "People! I want at least five quitters! And I want them now!"

No one moves.

"I know - and you know - we all don't want to be here. That's okay, men. Not everyone has to be here. I've got the day room all warmed up. You can cuddle up with a blanket and watch *Ryan's Hope* and *Days of Our Lives*."

Everyone tries to hold back their laughter.

"All right! If that's the way you want it. Front Leaning Rest position. Move!"

Cory and about four hundred airborne trainees hit the ground. Their hands rest in the gravel as they stand by to do probably a million push-ups.

"In cadence. Exercise! One, two, three - One! One, two, three - Two!"

Simultaneously, all four hundred men push up and down.

They yell, "One!...Two!...Three!" with every other push-up.

The Black Hats spread out into the ranks looking to harass the weak. They get down in their faces screaming. Chaos seems rampant. The First Sergeant continues until the fittest of soldiers are ready to collapse. To really push them, he holds them in the up position for what seems like an eternity. Cory's arms, back, and stomach scream in agony. He keeps concentrating, holding his eyes to the front. His body trembles with the strain. His hands sting from the gravel that pierces his palms.

Finally, the First Sergeant bellows, "On your feet!"

The harassment continues another fifteen

minutes. Push-ups, sit-ups, leg raises, and anything else he can come up with. As the First Sergeant starts calling for his quitters, three broken and ready to quit trainees step forward. They move quickly up the stairs to the First Sergeant. Their heads hang low and they feel ashamed. He whispers a few words to them, and then he sends them inside.

"I want more quitters!"

The formation of soon-to-be paratroopers is upset now. They are sick and tired of being harassed. A collective determination falls over the masses. Somewhere in the ranks of men, one man starts a beat. Like in the grand stand of any college football game, the chant gets louder and louder. The left foot hits the gravel, then the right, followed by one clap of hands.

"Boom! Boom! Cha! Boom! Boom! Cha! Boom! Boom! Cha!"

The sound echoes through the Army quad. Every soldier perfectly times the other. It grows louder and louder.

"Boom! Boom! Cha! Boom! Boom! Cha!"

The sound becomes deafening. The First Sergeant tilts his hat back on his head and grins watching the four hundred trainees. He nods his head in agreement, then he turns and walks back inside the barracks. The quad erupts with cheers of celebration. The First Sergeant is beaten. This time.

Through it all, Cory participates with a sense of awe for the collective spirit. He has never seen anything like it before.

All the quitters, all the soldiers too injured to continue, and all the guys that just couldn't cut the mustard, he has no sympathy for. In one way or another, they have brought failure on themselves. They aren't tough enough. It lifts his confidence knowing he has what it takes.

When it comes right down to it, everyone is out for themselves. He knows that. The trainees are in their third and final week. Dozens of troops have already disappeared from the ranks. But there will be more before graduation day. The Airborne wings worn above the left breast pocket are meant to be earned, not just given away.

Individual Black Hat instructors now form up their assigned platoons. It's time for the morning run. With each day, the length and speed increase. Anyone who falls more than two feet to the rear is pulled. Everyone must be able to handle the pace or they're gone. It's that simple.

Cory has become pretty good friends with his roommate. His name is Billy Johnson, but everyone calls him "Ears" instead. He looks a lot like Opie except his ears are about five times as big. With his required airborne trainee crew cut, he looks like a big egg with ears. For some reason, he likes his nickname, and so do the Black Hats who gave it to him.

"Hey Ears!" the Black Hat shouts looking at Billy through the ranks. "I've been told we're gonna have to give you a roll of duct tape."

"Sergeant?" Billy replies.

"I understand on the last jump, as soon as you exited the aircraft, your ears caused you a major malfunction. A spin out, to be exact!"

The troops find the exchange hilarious and everyone is laughing.

"So, we've decided to duct tape your ears down to the side of your head."

Everyone laughs again, including Billy. His optimism is contagious.

"Right face! Forward march!"

Cory and Billy march side by side down the street and into the parade field.

"A few more days," Billy says.

"Yeah. No sweat," replies Cory. "Try to keep up, huh?"

"I'll be right on your heels, McGuire."

"Double time! March!"

Like race horses out of the starting gate, they spring off. As the pace quickens, everyone in perfect unison, nothing is heard but feet hitting the ground. The Black Hat begins to sing a cadence and the trainees respond, repeating each phrase.

"C-130 rolling down the strip. Airborne Daddy gonna take a little trip."

"Stand up, hook up, shuffle to the door. Jump right out and count to four."

"If my chute don't open wide, I've got another one by my side."

"If that one should fail me too, look out ground I'm comin' through."

The pace quickens. They pass other platoons. Soldiers are strewn all over both sides of the road collapsed or throwing up. The Black Hats yell at people to keep up.

It's not working, and Cory's guys are falling out to the side. Soldiers shout to each other.

"Come on! Come on! Don't fall out! Hang in there!"

Billy goes after one guy. Cory sees him.

"No! Let him go! He can't hang! Get back here!"

Billy returns to the formation watching the soldier stumble and fall.

"Are you crazy or what?" Cory asks him.

"I just wanted to help."

"Help yourself!" Cory replies angrily.

Billy looks at him with a frown.

A total of ten soldiers fall out of the run and they've covered at least seven miles. The Black Hat brings the platoon to a halt in front of the barracks and dismisses them. Cory stands for a moment to catch his breath. He bends over, puts his hands on his knees and breathes deeply.

Billy, in much better condition, stays with him. Cory stands straight and slowly rotates his arm as if his shoulder is stiff.

"How's the shoulder?" Billy asks.

Cory is surprised by his observation. "Fine. Not a problem."

Since the Black Hats will do anything to find quitters, Cory isn't giving them any reason to weed him out. Broken arms and legs help the selection process a lot. Nobody that wants to stay goes to sick call. They might as well sign their quitter papers beforehand.

Cory's seen soldiers stitching up other soldiers, bandaging arms and legs, and popping anti-inflammatory pills. The unspoken rule requires that if a man is injured, he must suck it up and drive on.

"Has the swelling gone down any?"

"Look, it's fine, okay?" Cory bends down

to retie his shoe which doesn't need it.

"It's just that-" Billy begins.

"It's just that what?" Cory snaps. "That I'm hurt and you're not? That I got a jacked-up arm and you don't? Or, maybe, you just feel sorry for me. Well, guess what? I don't need your sympathy. I can handle a little twinge in my shoulder."

Cory takes a deep breath and calms down. "It's really not a big deal. I just landed a little wrong last week. It's better now. Don't worry about me, okay?"

"You practically dislocated your shoulder, Cory."

"Yeah, yeah. Well, I guess only the tough survive. You're my hero," Cory snarls again.

"I just thought-"

"Look. It's not your problem. I can handle it."

Billy, now angered by Cory's attitude, jabs him in the arm so they're eye to eye. "Look, Buddy. Whether you know it or not you haven't been doing *anything* alone. When you couldn't lift your arm five inches, who do you think was helping you out?"

"What are you talking about?" Cory asks, his eye narrowing.

"I'm talking about the push-ups and everything else. I'm talking about getting the guys to sound off to muffle your scream. I'm talking about moving around so the Black Hats wouldn't spot you. That's what I'm talking about."

With that, Billy turns and storms away. Cory puts another knot in his shoe lace and watches Billy's retreating back.

Graduation day arrives, and the parade field is filled with bleachers, flags, bands, and soldiers in their Class-A uniforms. The General stands at the podium and gives the speech he gives every graduation.

Families sit in the stands waving to their individual soldiers and wiping tears with handkerchiefs. Cory almost flinches remembering his last trip home and the father who couldn't be bothered to meet him at the airport, but quickly stuffs that memory away.

The ceremony lasts about a half an hour, and then the Black Hats hand out the coveted silver airborne wings.

"Congratulations, Airborne."

Cory and Billy receive their wings with the rest of the paratroopers. They march back to the barracks.

On the way Back, Cory realizes he's found the type of Army he's been looking for – everyone in their Class-A's marching strong and proud. And in his thoughts, he reminds himself that this is what being a real soldier is all about. These are the guys who can be trusted to fight alongside of. He wished all the Army could be like this.

The formation comes to a halt, and the First Sergeant stands at the top of the stairs.

"Blood wings will be administered directly following this formation. Dismissed!"

"Hey, Ears! You going with me?" Cory asks Billy.

"Nah. It's not my thing."

"What do you mean it's not your thing? You're Airborne now, right?" Cory smiles wide.

Billy shrugs. "I'm still Airborne without the Blood Wings."

"Suit yourself. I'll see ya after." Cory goes inside the barracks with a few other enthusiastic guys.

He raps on the door and it's almost ripped off the hinges when it's jerked open.

"What do you want, Airborne?" the soldier demands.

"Blood Wings, Sergeant," Cory replies.

"Get in here!"

In the small office, Black Hats are busy talking, reading reports, talking on the phone, and doing other miscellaneous administrative chores. The soldiers spread out. The atmosphere is chaotic again.

"Come here, you!" shouts the Black Hat pointing at Cory.

The one who picked Cory is a thin wiry type. When he raises his voice, the pitch goes higher and higher.

"So, you want Blood Wings, huh?"

He adjusts a pair of metal airborne wings above Cory's right breast pocket. Cory can already feel the two long pointed barbs poking him in the chest.

Cory, highly motivated shouts, "Yes, Sergeant!"

The funny looking Black Hat really draws out the moment. With everything he's got, he slams Cory's chest with the palm of his hand. Cory rockets across the room hitting the back wall. Pictures go crashing to the floor. Cory's head hits the wall and he slides down onto a couch. The wind is knocked out of him and he can't feel the pain of the wings which are embedded in his chest.

"What are you doing?" one of the Black Hats says to Cory's tormenter as the room goes silent.

"Giving him Blood Wings."

"Well you don't have to kill him doing it!"

The other airborne troopers swallow hard at the sight of Cory. Cory stands up awkwardly and shakes it off, acting like it didn't faze him. Never pulling the barbs from his chest, he turns to leave.

"Thanks, Sarge," he says coolly, looking the soldier in the eye.

Billy meets Cory at the bottom of the stairs. "How'd it go?"

"Perfect," Cory says.

He looks over his shoulder. Then he goes to pull the wings out of his chest.

"Hey. Let me give you a hand," Billy says quietly.

"I got it," Cory snaps, slapping Billy's arm away. Then, as though Billy is nothing more than a passing acquaintance, he says, "Maybe I'll look you up sometime when I'm down at Fort Bragg. You're going to the 82nd, right?"

Billy waits a second and then nods. "Yeah, Cory. The 82nd."

There's an uncomfortable pause then Billy winks at him. "De Oppresso Liber, right?"

Cory's confused. "Huh?"

"You know, freedom for the oppressed? Green Berets? Special Forces? Remember?"

"Oh yeah! Right. De Oppresso Liber." Cory's beginning to feel like a fool, but he's not even sure why.

"Take care, Cory," Billy calls over his shoulder as he walks away.

Cory stares after him. "See ya, Billy."

* * *

At the barracks Cory packs his gear. He takes one last look at his room and then pushes through the door. With his duffel bag hanging over his shoulder, he passes all the soldiers with their families.

They take pictures, kiss, and hug one another. Cory zig zags through them and boards a waiting troop bus. He finds a seat and stares out the window at the families as the bus pulls away.

CHAPTER FIVE

SMALL COMMERCIAL AIRPORT - DAY

   With Airborne School complete, Cory is on
his way to Fort Bragg. His plane glides
into Fayetteville, North Carolina in
February and the tensions in the Middle
East and the Gulf are well established.

   Walking through the small airport, out of
the corner of his eye, Cory sees a CNN
report on a television in the airport
lounge. From the arrival corridor, he
watches. A couple guys in uniform drinking
beer and smoking cigarettes sit oblivious
to the news on the screen. They've no doubt
seen it a hundred times before. They laugh
and joke about one thing or another.

Another man on a pay phone has a finger in his ear so he can hear his call. His son stares at the screen from below. He points and tries to get his daddy's attention. The man waves him off, obviously annoyed.

Cory watches the war-like actions of Iraq's president Saddam Hussein. Tanks maneuver all over the country threatening their Arab neighbors. He wonders for a moment how he might fit into all this, then grabs his duffel bag and finds taxi cab drivers outside the airport biding for fares. An elderly black man, tall and large around the waist, grabs Cory's bag and charms him into his taxi.

With a thick accent, he says, "Fort Bragg, right?"

"That's right," Cory replies.

"Twenty one-dollar bills and you be right at the front door, my man."

"Fifteen?" Cory counters.

"Come on now, I got to make a living here. Eighteen dollars and I'll carry your duffel bag anywhere you want to go, my man," the cabbie says with a wide grin.

"Okay, okay. But I'll carry the duffel bag," Cory concedes.

"No sweat, my man," the driver says as he sinks deep into his seat and clicks over the meter.

They drive off. After a few minutes, he adjusts his review mirror to see Cory better.

"You Eighty Second?"

"Nope," Cory says.

The taxi driver starts humming a church tune. He thinks of something else to say.

"You goin' to Coscom?"

"No," Cory says, irritated by his prying. Deducing it will probably continue, Cory volunteers some information. "I'm reporting to Special Forces school."

"Uh huh. My man be going all the way then?"

Cory thinks about that. "As far as I can," he says.

"I'm twenty-year man myself. Retired with Supply Corps. I did the Nam, my man. Ain't no messin' around in that. It was the real deal!" He pauses to reflect. "Tell you what. You find out something about yourself in combat, my man."

Cory's slow to answer. "What's that?"

He glances at Cory through the rear-view mirror. "What you is-and what you ain't."

Cory searches his mind seeking understanding.

"When those bullets be flyin' and those bombs be busting all around killin' your brothers, you learn something," the driver says with a quiet intensity. He pauses again. Speaking as if to himself, he says, "What you think you is, you ain't. And what you think you ain't, you is."

Somehow, the man's simple words strike Cory profoundly. He isn't quite sure what it means, but, somehow, he knows it is a truth. He's knows it's for him.

The taxi moves onto Fort Bragg. It looks like any other Army base. The taxi driver points things out along the way, like a tour guide in New York City.

"And that over there be the Special Forces Museum."

Cory asks, "What's that in the middle of

the grass?"

Pointing, the cabbie says, "Green Beret statue."

Cory says, "Stop here for a second."

Cory steps out of the taxi and walks across the lawn. He stands there, looking up at a large bronze statue of a Green Beret dressed in a Vietnam-era combat uniform. On his head is a green beret, and in his hand, he carries an M-16 rifle. He stands poised, focused, and professional.

Cory experiences a second of exhilaration. His destiny is practically in his hands. He can almost picture graduation day. He recalls what he remembers about the force and the elite Special Forces, Green Berets. They are the best. Each candidate is selected for his special qualities. They must be survivors willing to complete the mission at any cost. They can infiltrate enemy territory virtually undetected. From advanced hand to hand combat to learning to survive alone off the land, they are trained to fight and survive anytime and anywhere. Indeed, a special breed of soldier.

Cory stays a moment longer and then returns to the taxi. He jumps inside, and they're gone. After a few minutes, the taxi pulls in front of the barracks where Cory is to report in. It's Friday and Special Forces Assessment and Selection, also known as SFAS, does not start until Monday morning.

Getting out of the taxi, Cory hands the driver a twenty-dollar bill and tells him to keep the change. He takes five steps, then swings around on his heel to the taxi driver.

"Say, what did you do in Nam, anyway?"

The elderly black man shook his head. "Nha Trang, 1969."

With that, he pulls away with a wave. Cory watches him drive off.

Cory smiled. "Sure, buddy," he whispered.

CHAPTER SIX

FORT BRAGG DEMONSTRATION FIELD - DAY

At the same time, and unknown to Cory, on the other side of Fort Bragg there was a lot going on.

"Wop! Wop! Wop!"

The whirling chopper blades of a Black Hawk helicopter are heard in the distance. The Jungle-like foliage is green and plush. Screaming low overhead, the Black Hawk emerges over the tree line, makes a hard banking turn, and stops in mid-flight.

Before it begins an even hover, long ropes descend rapidly from the open door-ports. Men on either side, one on top of the other, slide fast-roping-quick to the bottom. They land on the roof of a two-story cement building. Their weapons swivel continuously covering all directions of fire. Like a machine, rehearsed over and over again, a door charge is set, and it explodes.

The men rush in. The sounds of single and short burst automatic fire can be heard. Small flash bang charges echo, lighting up the building. A few men rappel from the sides of the roof swinging fast into windows below. Organized communication can be heard. The weapons fire continues through the rooms on each floor. Smoke billows out the top floor windows.

In less than a few minutes, the team of men dashes out the main floor entrance carrying the hostages. The men form a protective perimeter around the Black Hawk which has just descended adjacent the smoldering building. The red smoke thrown prior signals that the mission is complete. It whirls in the wind from the chopper blades.

Each man, one by one, moves in and onto

the aircraft without a wasted motion. At almost the same time as lift off, the Black Hawk makes a sharp banking turn and screams away. A tremendous explosion follows as the cement building shakes and rumbles from the delayed charge left behind.

In a small set of bleachers, a crowd of people applaud in their dark suits and dresses. VIP's flags wave in the wind and generals sit nearby, pointing and explaining. Every face smiles for the adventure they've just witnessed.

Amidst the extended applause, the Black Hawk helicopter returns and slowly sets down, cutting its engines. Swiftly the team files out and forms a single rank in front of the helicopter.

Standing before the audience, eight Green Berets stand at attention. On their heads they wear their green berets. Their boots are spit shined and their fatigues are starched from head to toe. The group of onlookers, escorted by colonels and generals in class-A uniforms, approach the team. The team commander takes one step to the front.

"Captain John Granger. Commander, Operational Detachment 792."

The next man in line steps forward. "Sergeant First Class Mike Berry. Senior Weapons Sergeant. Operational Detachment 792."

One by one they step forward and identify themselves.

"Staff Sergeant Jose Ortiz. Junior Communications Sergeant. Operational Detachment 792."

"Sergeant First Class James Wilson. Senior Engineer Sergeant. Operational Detachment 792."

The ritual goes on and the VIP demonstration serves its purpose. The generals and other high-up brass congratulate the team's solid performance.

And in the near distance, a single mock building sits smoldering in the late afternoon sun.

CHAPTER SEVEN

AUDITORIUM - DAY

   At exactly 0900 hours Monday morning,
Cory and the other SFAS candidates file
into the auditorium. In an orderly fashion,
approximately two-hundred and eighty
soldiers fill row upon row. Wearing their
fatigues, they stand at Attention.

   All name tags and unit identification are
stripped. The only thing to identify them
is a hastily sewn strip of cloth above
their right top pocket which bares the
markings of their new identification. With
black indelible ink, Cory has written the
number "76." He is no longer a soldier in
training, but, rather, a number being

evaluated. For three weeks, this will be who he is. The hall remains silent. After a few moments, an order is called out.

"Attention!"

To the podium, strolls the colonel in charge of the Special Forces Assessment and Selection. "Take your seats, men," he says casually.

As if a single unit, the numbered soldiers take their seats. In his green beret and starched fatigues, he looks at the faces before him.

"Welcome to SFAS, men. For the next three weeks, you will be evaluated on your performances. Since you are meeting with me here today, it means you have met several demanding prerequisites. Congratulations. But by no means have you made it yet."

He slowly paces the stage. "Roughly sixty-five to seventy percent of you won't make it. SFAS is designed to seek out the soldiers with the type of character most epitomizing the Green Beret. No matter what, you are all undoubtedly fine soldiers. Perhaps, though, not the type we are looking for.

"As you may have noticed in your welcome packets there is a lack of specific criteria given for this course. It is our mission to see how you will react in any given combat situation. To do this, we must achieve an environment commensurate to that of actual combat. Therefore, as is most often the case in combat, you will not be given a schedule of events. You will, however, be deprived of sleep, food, and shelter. We will push your body's endurance levels to the utmost extremes. You will spend many hours alone. We want to see what makes you tick. We want to take the wrapping off and see what's inside.

"In this next three weeks, we will find out who you really are. We will know you better than you know yourselves. This process is not one-hundred-percent fool proof, but it's dang close. No single person is going to help you through. You will be forced to rely on yourselves. Men, if it was easy, we wouldn't be the elite force we are today."

He pauses. He stops and faces the frozen faces before him. Looking them over for a moment, he continues.

"Look to your left and look to your right. Chances are that man won't be with you three weeks from now. You have come here from all different walks of life. Not by fate, but rather by choice. You all have your own individual reasons for wanting to be here. Some of you don't want to be here but you just don't know it yet. And after you have given everything you've got, finding you can go no further, the man that reaches deep down into his soul pulling out the source which keeps his desires burning is the man who will be able to complete the mission. These are the men we want in Special Forces - ones willing to go the distance, no matter what. Good luck, men."

"On your feet!" a voice cries out as the colonel swiftly makes an exit. The candidates slowly file out.

* * *

PHYSICAL TRAINING TEST SITE - QUARTER MILE TRACK - PRE-DAWN

"One! One! One! Soldier, your chest must make contact with the ground. One! One! Lock those elbows. Three! Three! Back straight! Back straight! Six! Seven! Eight!"

With Cory desperately attempting his best push-ups, a Green Beret evaluator kneeling next to him counts only the perfect ones.

It's 0600 hours. In the early morning darkness, the stadium is lit with overhead lights. Breath rising from the candidates creates an eerie pseudo-fog.

In what appears to be orderly chaos, the men stand in columns waiting their turns. A physical fitness test is being administered. Two-hundred and seventy points must be accumulated, and Cory is not looking so good. Wearing his Army gray sweats and red-numbered 76 bib, Cory vigorously pushes at the earth. His arms are moving like pistons as he starts to get into an even rhythm. The column of troops behind him look on as the grader now counts each of his push-ups. He has to do as many as he can in two minutes.

"You have fifteen seconds remaining. Sixty-seven! Sixty-eight!"

Cory forces his exhausted arms to push once more. "Sixty-nine and seventy! Time!"

Cory stands. His arms feel like rubber and his head pounds. He moves to the back of the line to wait his next turn.

The evaluator hadn't counted at least twenty of his push-ups and that bothered him. He wondered why. In all the time he'd been in the Army, with all the PT tests he'd taken along the way, he never produced a bad push-up. Well, at least, not until now.

Cory has three more events to finish: sit-ups for two minutes, a two-mile timed run, and a fifty-meter swim test in fatigues and boots.

The other guys are faring about the same. They are being shorted. Occasionally, a candidate complains as he continues the exercise. They all had to do well or go home.

Cory is in good condition and he knows it. He's trained for months before coming.

And now he's being cheated. Again, Cory does his sit-ups, but only sixty-two of them count.

The two-mile run is next.

* * *

As the men finish the push-ups and sit-ups, they head to the quarter-mile track. Candidates jump up and down trying to stay warm. Tall lengthy marathon-types stretch for the record times they are going to set. It looks like the Olympic tryouts.

The massive group of soldiers is split into three sections. Cory stands at the starting line with the first heap. The narrow track is stuffed with runners. As Cory stands at the ready, he wonders how they can cheat him on this event.

"Go!" the evaluator with the stop watch says.

The runners spring from the starting line. Eight laps are needed for the two-mile requirement. Cory will choke up a lung if he has to get a 12:45 minute time. He stays close to the inside as he rounds the first corner. Runners with their bibs flying in the wind, bump off one another as they try to stay to the inside. Gravel is flying in every direction. Cory rounds his first lap.

"1:25!" the evaluator shouts.

The runners start to spread out. Cory goes into his own world. He hears only the pounding of his heart and sees his hands rocketing up and down. His concentration sends him even deeper. The once-thundering storm of runners around him becomes a muffled whisper. He turns another lap.

"3:01!"

His breaths are heavy and fast. Streams of sweat fall into his eyes burning them. "I got to push it. I got to push it. Come on..." he grunts to himself.

He thinks about the episode of push-ups and sit-ups. His arms rocket faster. A burning sensation grips his lungs. His legs ache for oxygen. He pushes harder, thinking *faster, faster*.

"5:09!"

His heart races, feeling as if it will explode. He makes another lap, then another. Stretching it out, he passes runners like a blur.

"11:58!"

His final lap.

He gasps for air. There is none. The arms, legs, and calves scream out in pain threatening to stop him in his tracks. As if each stride is his last, he stretches. Blood from his lungs rises to his throat.

No air! No air! Like pure salt in his eyes, the sweat burns. Rounding another turn, the blood pounds in his head. The last turn.

Go! Go! Go! he tells himself. *I need air! I need air!* his body screams. He pushes it.

"12:47! 48! 49! Time!"

Cory stumbles past the evaluator who clicks the stop watch. Unable to catch his breath, with his hands on his hips, Cory stumbles about as his legs and lungs fight to catch up.

As quickly as they left him, the sights and sounds around him return. His survivor state of mind is gone. He is no longer alone surviving another questionable outcome.

The time he scored is good enough. He isn't sure about the push-ups and sit-ups.

Cory's heart rate returns to normal and his breathing eases. Candidates all around him are busy recovering. Some just stand with their heads hanging. Others lay on the ground, sending deep breathes steamily into the crisp February morning. Some are vomiting and others, red-faced, pace back and forth.

They have given it their all. Runners continue to cross the finish line. Cory finds himself thinking about the next event. He takes a deep breath and looks skyward. The sun is beginning to rise and in the bright stadium lights he observes the insects colliding off one another as they fight for the heat and light.

* * *

Later at the swim test: Drip! Drip! Drip! Soaked fatigues send drops of water off Cory's trouser legs and into his boots. At the edge of the lengthy indoor pool the candidates stand waiting their turn. A quick and cold rinsing is required before going in.

Eight at a time are sent down the length of the pool. In their heavy fatigues and boots, they struggle across and back again. Evaluators stand on the sides with lifeguard poles at their ready. A kid gets about half-way across the pool. He desperately tries to keep his head above water. He starts to panic. He swims frantically but goes nowhere.

The candidates spread around the pool begin to shout. "Come on! Come on! You can do it!" The sound echoes throughout.

"Shut up! Shut up! There will be no assistance given. Leave him alone," an evaluator shouts over the cheers.

Everything goes silent and only the desperate attempts to get air, and the thrashing of water can be heard. The kid tires and finally begins to sink for the last time. His last outstretched hand slowly goes under. The atmosphere is tense, and the lifeguards wait. Until the last possible moment, they wait.

Finally, one of them casually sends his long pole after the drowning candidate. Grabbing the end, the kid emerges above the surface gasping for air. The pole is brought in and the candidate crawls onto the edge of the pool, exhausted.

He's gone and Cory knows it. Just like that. Although Cory is a great swimmer, he can't help but worry. The evaluator points to the next group of men and Cory jumps in the pool. Holding on to the edge of the pool, he can feel the weight and drag of his fatigues.

The evaluator stands at the end of the diving board and says, "Release."

Cory lets go and starts to kick and use his arms to stay afloat. The Evaluator first checks for coherency in the eyes of each man. After a moment, feeling satisfied of this, he says, "Begin!"

Cory remains calm. In fact, he feels quite confident. He breast-strokes to the end of the pool, and without touching the edge, turns around. As he swims, he takes long controlled stokes sending his body purposefully gliding under water. He raises his head and grabs some more air. Even with the boots and fatigues, he swims easily.

Next to him, a soldier is struggling horribly. Wild-eyed with terror, the soldier's eyes meet Cory's. He grabs frantically to hold on and Cory is halted. Once again, their eyes meet. Cory understands that look of desperation. He's seen it before in another man's eyes. A man he called his father.

For a moment, he hesitates. For an instant, he's frozen.

Then he grips the soldier's hand and rips it off his arm. With one kick, Cory skillfully glides away leaving the young man sinking behind him. Cory gets to the end of the pool.

The evaluator checks for coherency again. He gives him a thumbs-out of the pool. As Cory looks behind him, he sees the soldier kneeling at the edge of the pool coughing up water. Long strands of saliva hang from his mouth.

He turns his head and looks at Cory. Cory

stands looking back for a moment, then turns away. A couple of guys secretly pat him on the back as he walks by. Nothing would ever be said about performances during the three weeks at SFAS.

CHAPTER EIGHT

IN A MILITARY TRANSPORT TRUCK - EARLY
MORNING - RAIN

The next day after the rest of the
prerequisites were completed, the heavy
canvas snaps in the wind as the standard
Army 2 1/2-ton cargo truck rumbles down the
road and out of Fort Bragg.

In the back of the Deuce and a Half, Cory
sits with the other candidates. The winter
air rushing in makes them cringe. Their
collars are flipped up as they grip the two
ends to keep the chill out. The falling
rain sprays a heavy mist inside the back of
the truck.

Across from Cory, Number Ninety-eight
watches him. With brown hair, a dark

mustache, and dark green eyes, he stares. Although a couple of years older than Cory, his weight and build are about the same. He leans back in the bench seat and puts a boot up on a rucksack.

"Hey! Seventy-six!"

"Yeah?" Cory says looking him in the eye.

"That boy almost took you down yesterday."

"Yep."

"You were pretty lucky, I figure."

Cory sits erect, suddenly feeling challenged.

"Oh? How do you figure?"

Number Ninety-eight looks out the back of the truck. "I don't know, but I think you do." He looks back at Cory. "Maybe, don't get so close to others, ya know?"

Cory nods his head and looks down the road. After a lengthy pause, he says, "This ain't combat, candidate."

"Ain't it?" Number Ninety-eight replies.

Cory glares at him.

Number Ninety-eight shrugs. "Hey, I just thought I'd try and help out a little," he says with a smart aleck smile.

Cory, wanting to lighten it up little, grins back.

* * *

The big troop carrier bumps along the highway. Camp Mackall is about an hour and a half away. The countryside has become more and more dense. With vegetation of all sorts, they cross over one long rolling hill after another.

Short, woody pine trees make up the countryside. The gates to the small compound open as the convoy of trucks approach.

Camp Mackall is isolated from most soldiers and sits alone amidst the dense North Carolina landscape. As the rain continues to pour, Cory spots rows of crudely built troop huts. A tall cyclone fence with rolling strands of concertina wire encircles the compound. Like some primitive special operations base camp, Camp Mackall fits the bare necessities image perfectly.

Clothes hang on lines despite the

drenching rain. Three spigots rise from the ground and tin wash pans lay about. Mostly sand and gravel cover the ground with an occasional crop of weeds. To one corner of the compound, a row of old Jeeps and trailers sit.

Although the camp seems primitive and somewhat deserted, Cory feels it also possesses a sense of purpose.

The trucks come to a stop in the middle of the compound and the tailgates drop. Candidates begin to off-load. Cory jumps off the truck with his gear. It takes mere seconds for the ice-cold rain to drench him. Soldiers move quickly, shouting to get organized. Cory picks up his gear and starts moving toward what he thinks to be the formation area.

A couple of guys shout, "Formation! Formation!"

Cory drops something as he starts moving out.

"Hey!" a candidate says as he stoops to pick up the dropped object.

Cory turns around.

"You might need these, Airborne!" The man straightens, holding the articles outstretched.

"Billy is that you?"

"In the flesh, my friend."

Cory, totally confused, stammers, "But I thought—?"

Billy's smile faded. "You never asked."

"You got to be kidding me."

"Now would I kid about something like this?" Billy holds his arms outstretched in the driving rain.

"Why didn't I see you earlier?"

"I had to come on advance party yesterday. I kind of got volunteered, ya know?"

Unable to make any real sense of the whole thing, Cory continues. "Are you sure you know what you're doing?"

Billy wipes the rain out of his eyes and nose. "Well, I'm here, ain't I?"

"Yeah, but I don't know Billy. I just never figured you the type."

"The world's full of all kinds, huh,

Cory?"

Cory stares for a moment studying Billy. He notices his short wiry figure, his droopy, sagging fatigues and the water splashing off his huge ears. "Yeah, I guess so."

"Hey! We better get to formation. Do you want these or not?" Billy holds out a set of dog tags.

"Oh man! Thanks." Cory whistles, shaking his head.

Cory and Billy dash to formation. The candidates stand four rows deep. The rain continues to pound. Cory looks around, and in the ranks, sees a variety of soldiers ranging from large to small, tall to short, some younger and some older. Then he remembers the Colonel's speech that the candidates come from all over. Since the PT test and the swim test, he notices how the ranks have already thinned. As he stands at attention, his fingers start to go numb, and he wonders if anyone else's are.

* * *

A Green Beret evaluator comes out of the

head shed and slowly walks to the front of the formation. Seemingly unaware of the rain, he walks up smiling.

"Welcome to Camp Mackall Special Forces Assessment and Selection Facility. This is really easy, Guys. You have a chalkboard on that tree over there," he points. "Everything you need to know will be written on it. You will check it as many times as you have to. No one will remind you of anything. That board is your instructions. Follow them to the letter. Pay attention to detail. Do not miss anything. Do not ask any of the evaluators or cadre any questions.

"We are not here to lead you or supervise you. We are not here to train you or advise you. It's all up to you. We are here to just simply monitor and evaluate you. If you get injured, if you are ill, if you become a heat casualty, or hypothermic, you can see a medic. If you need further medical assistance, you are not gonna get it here. You will have to VW - "voluntarily withdrawal" – from Selection. We only provide basic first aid here.

"If you want to finish, you're just gonna have to suck it up and drive on. Your rack time will be limited. Sleep is not a luxury you can afford here. You will be issued one MRE, "Meals Ready-to-Eat," a day. Do not let fatigue and the lack of supervision get the best of you. Never deviate from basic soldiering rules and regulations. We see a lot of guys get tired and forget.

"If you leave your weapon, if you are more than an arms-length away from it, you are wrong. No one is going to correct you. If it is seen happening, it will be written up with your roster number. To put this in terms you can all understand, if you are late, if you cheat, if you lie, if you lose anything, if you make a mistake, if you run out of water, if you do not follow the instructions on the board exactly, you most likely will not be selected come Selection Day. It pays to be a winner here.

"We are an equal opportunity employer though. We give you as much slack as you need to fail or succeed."

He pauses and looks out into the ranks as the rain still pours. "And some of you don't want to be here. You just don't know it yet."

Finishing his speech, he wastes no time. "Now, fall out and pick up your meal which is in the box." He points to a large cardboard box of MRE's. "Move out to your assigned huts. Check the board at 1900 hours for your first instructions. Move out!"

* * *

In his hut, Cory finds ten bunk beds. Five to each side. It's barren except for the cold cement floor and the mattress-less steel bunk frames.

Cory moves to an empty bunk and begins organizing his equipment. He rolls a sleeping bag down the length of the bunk. He looks around and sees guys checking the comfort of the springs. No one complains. This is part of what they will be tested on: their ability to deal with the lack of comfort.

Cory lies gingerly on his bunk testing its comfort. There is no comfort, just squeaky springs sticking in his back. The job of SFAS is to make you feel as uncomfortable as possible all the time.

Can they take it? That's what it comes down to. After a while, the ones that can't will eventually blow a fuse and end up quitting. This suits Cory just fine. He wants to see each man tested. If they can't take it, then good. They don't belong, and Special Forces will get only the best.

* * *

A short thin Italian kid is lying in the bunk next to Cory. His blood shot eyes bulge and his rough five o' clock shadow gives him a sloppy, unfit appearance. Soaked to the bone with his hands behind his head, he stares at the bunk springs above him.

"It's cold ain't it?" he says in a thick New Jersey accent.

Cory looks around and figures he must be

talking to him, so he shrugs. "It's supposed to be."

"Yeah, guess so. Albert. Nice to meet you, okay?" He extends a hand to shake.

"Cory McGuire." Cory shakes his hand. Then both settle back into their bunks.

"You Seventy-six? I'm Roster Number One-hundred. It's a good number to have, I think. Lucky, you know?"

"Strong number, Albert."

"Kind of high profile though. Don't know if I like that."

"You a little nervous, Albert?"

"Who me? I don't think so." A pause. "Well, maybe a little." He holds up a couple fingers showing about an inch between. A long pause follows, and they just stare at the springs above them. "Ya know, a lot of guys don't make it."

"That's what they tell me," Cory replies.

Another pause. "I got to make it, man. You never hear what happens out here, though."

"What do you mean?" Cory says feeling a bit more interested.

"What? You ain't heard?"

"No."

"They got boys dyin' out here. A candidate died of heat stroke last cycle. In January, no less. Man, it happens all the time. Boys be walkin' around with both lungs full of pneumonia and drop somewhere out there."

"I never heard, but I guess anything's possible."

Albert, somewhat worked up now, continues. "I mean, they let you *die* out here!" Another pause.

"You got to want it," Cory says softly, as if to himself. Another pause.

"They're gonna try and hurt us, McGuire."

"Yeah, I know. But this is just something I need to do."

"You mean prove?"

"No," says Cory. "Do!"

Albert shrugs. "If you say so."

"Let me give you some advice, Albert. Don't let them break you. Play the game, be what they're looking for. Survivor-type, you know?"

"Surviving's one thing. Dyins' another."

A candidate walks by with his sleeping bag draped over his shoulder.

"Better not get caught lying in those racks."

Cory and Albert fly up and out of their bunks.

CHAPTER NINE

CAMP MACKALL - DAWN

The early morning is cool and crisp. The rain has stopped, and the clouds disappeared sometime the night before. With a fresh new day at hand, Selection Phase is underway. The one-and-a-half-mile obstacle course waits.

In the woods behind the compound, odd structures are sprawled about. Two hundred some odd candidates are following Green Berets who are giving them walk-throughs.

"This obstacle is called the 'Dirty Name.' You must maneuver over the first horizontal log, jump to the second higher one and then to the third, flip over the top, then down to the ground. Then move out quickly to the next obstacle." They walked to the next one.

"This is the 'Leg Breaker.' Any questions?"

Six ropes ascend sixty feet, tied to a horizontal log. Ropes descend from the log at an arching angle back to the ground. As the exhausted candidates reach the top of the first rope, they usually fall trying to switch to the second rope. A fitting nickname because of the injuries it causes. They move to the next obstacle.

"This is the 'Executioner.'" A rope ascends twenty feet to a horizontal log. The candidate must climb the rope, flip on top of the log, stand up and step over to another log. From there a log rises, extending the over-all height another fifteen feet. The log thins drastically as it rises. From there, a rickety ladder is fastened horizontally, and the candidate has to walk across the rungs which rise another ten feet. A rope is strung horizontally at the other end. The soldier must maneuver along that rope to another rope which drops to the ground.

"This over here is called the 'B Buster!', and with the rain yesterday, these logs are as slick as snot."

Long telephone poles rise at an angle. At about twenty feet an adjoining log meets it. As the candidates run up the log, the log width thins out, making it virtually impossible to make the switch.

The group goes through the rest of the obstacle course, being shown obstacles with names like the "Terminator," "Dead Man's Jump," the "Spine Tingler," "Charlotte's Web," and the "Back Breaker."

The grotesque tour takes an hour. Ropes, nets, logs, and ditches are in every direction, around every corner. For what should be a simple test of confidence and coordination, a lot of medical vehicles are present.

Cory finds his place in line. Billy isn't too far in front of him. The red bibs bearing their roster numbers show brightly against their dark fatigues. Cory's heart starts to pound with anticipation. He thinks about the slick logs and obstacles like the "Leg Breaker."

Billy looks back down the line of men and sees Cory. He gives a big smile from big ear to big ear and waves like he's standing in line for a carnival ride. The evaluator clicks his stop watch and moves the first man through.

"Go!"

At one-minute intervals, the candidates are released into the events. As the line moves along, Cory starts shaking his legs and arms out. The closer he gets to the start line, the more he withdraws into his own world. All the sights and sounds around him begin to vanish until he's alone in his own world of survival. Cory gets to the front of the line.

"Roster Number Seventy-six, go!"

Cory dashes past the evaluator and the candidates behind him look on. He quickly high-steps thirty hurdles to his front. A man to his right slips and falls. Cory moves on, running as fast as he can around a corner and jumps onto the monkey bars. He swings rung by rung. About halfway he slips off. There's grease on the bar. He runs back to the start, picks up some dirt and soils his hands. An evaluator writes in his note book.

Cory power-grips each rung as he rockets to the other side. Already winded, he hops from log to log on the next obstacle, leap-frogging across.

He darts to "The Leg Breaker." He watches a candidate crash to the ground screaming in pain. An evaluator stands over him and calmly asks if he wants to attempt the obstacle again.

Cory leaps onto the rope and, hand over hand, climbs to the top. Another candidate to his right goes sliding down the rope burning his hands. Hands aching with pain, Cory lunges for the cross-over rope and swings his legs onto it. He slides as quickly as he can to the bottom. He looks at the evaluator, who waves him on.

Sweat rolls down his face and into his eyes as he charges to the next obstacle.

Another rope rises fifty feet straight up. Men stand hunched over trying to catch their breath. Cory leaps, wraps his feet to give more pulling power and pulls hand over hand. He can't make it up.

Billy goes scrambling to the top and back down again. Cory slides down. Men all around him attempt and re-attempt, each making it about five feet each time.

Cory looks at the evaluator, exhausted.

"Will you be attempting this obstacle again?" he's asked.

Cory looks at the other soldiers' failing attempts and says, "No!"

"Move out, Seventy-six!"

Cory runs to the next rope. A soldier stands frozen on "The Executioner's" ladder. Cory sees Billy skillfully dart by on the adjacent ladder. He feels a surge of power come over him. His focus becomes more intense. He grabs the rope.

A soldier falls from above him. He bounces hard off a log and crashes to the ground. Cory hears the snap of his arm when it breaks. Cory yells a motivated cry. The medics sit on the hood of their ambulances watching.

He pulls himself over the log. Breathing heavy, he starts feeling dizzy. He skirts to the adjoining log and ascends to the top. With his arms outstretched, he maintains his balance. He looks down. With one shaky step after another, he walks across the ladder. He slides down the rope and to the bottom.

Cory stumbles, crashes to the ground and then gets up. He bolts to the next obstacle and slides onto the ground on his stomach. Flipping over onto his back, he pistons his legs and arms. In the ditch under the one-foot-high barbed wire, he works his way out the other side.

A Green Beret stands in the woods observing him. Cory rolls to his feet and sees Billy running ahead of him. *He's having fun out here*, Cory thinks.

Billy smiles as he moves easily through each event. Cory wipes the blood, smearing it across his face.

Like a deer, Billy springs over the "B

Buster." Cory swallows hard. He runs fast to gain momentum and barely makes the thinning top of the log. He regains some balance and runs down the other side.

Cory keeps going. He's not sure if he can make it, but he keeps going anyway. He's winded and his head pounds. Every bone aches. He feels bruised and scratched from head to toe. Cory jumps on to the "Dirty Name" and quickly slides off. He tries again. He makes it up, gains his balance, and leaps to the next parallel bar. It meets him at his stomach. At about fifteen feet above the ground, he slowly stands on the thin bark-stripped pole. As he starts to lose his balance, he leaps to the high parallel bar and rolls over the other side. He drops, crashing to the bottom and rolls onto his feet. The evaluator waves him on.

Ahead of him, Billy is shouting and screaming like he's on a white-water rafting trip. "Woooooo! Yeeeeee hawwwwww!"

Cory leaps over the barbed wire mounds and moves to the cargo netting. "Charlotte's Web" has candidates captured and entangled. Cory follows Billy up the sixty-foot monstrosity. He grabs the woven ropes and vigorously pulls. Over the top, they go down the other side; first Billy then Cory.

Billy springs to the bottom and takes off running. Cory's fast behind him. He doesn't know what's keeping him going. Into a tunnel, they barrel as fast as they can. Soldier's screams and shouts echo in the chambers. In the darkness, Cory tries to feel his way. He crawls on his hands and knees and, after coming to an intersection he turns right.

A panicked candidate tears at him, screaming and angry. Cory moves by. He takes a left and crawls some more. Around the dark corner, he sees some light and moves toward it. As he reaches the opening, Cory grabs the rope and climbs out. His eyes ache from the brightness. He feels disoriented but starts running anyway. He's made it through the "Pit of darkness" a series of tunnels with any number of ways out. For some candidates, it is the *pit of their greatest fears.* Cory runs blindly for a moment. Billy is far ahead of him leaping and bounding effortlessly.

Cory is determined to catch him. Soaked with sweat, his face and fatigues are caked with dirt and grime. His knees and elbows bleed, as well as the cut from the barb wire on his face. He jogs his tired and beaten body to the next obstacle.

Candidates are strewn all around. Ambulance sirens can be heard. Some soldiers sit off to the sides too exhausted to continue. Cory stumbles and weaves by them. In front of him, the "Spine Tingler" awaits.

A Green Beret evaluator sits on a log and smiles at him. Cory knows what he's thinking and he's not about to give him the satisfaction of being right. Logs parallel each other, as they rise to form a huge triangle. Cory moves onto the obstacle, completely exhausted.

As he begins to weave his body through the logs, he sees blood smeared on the stripped logs. He grunts and pulls, contorting his body to slip through the narrow openings. His spine screams with pain as he manipulates his body through.

Nothing is going to stop him. Something inside him has taken over and he isn't going to give up. Knowing that he is disappointing the sadistic evaluator, he gets through the obstacle and spits the grime out of his mouth. He's beaten the trap and that will be his symbol of doing so. The evaluator scratches his chin and half-heartedly waves Cory on.

Dragging with each step and unable to get enough air, he pumps, pushes, and climbs his way over more obstacles. He lost sight of Billy somewhere around the Spine Tingler. At this point, he doesn't care where anyone is. He just wants to finish.

More tired than he can ever remember being, he sees nothing but his boots dragging along to the next obstacle. He makes a final lunge for what he can only guess to be another rope. He swings clear of a ditch full of water below him, and rolls onto the ground to a stop.

"Time! Roster Number Seventy-six!"
Cory is across the finish line.

CHAPTER TEN

CROSS COUNTRY TRAIL CAMP MACKALL - DAY

Blinded by the pounding rain, Cory runs. His boots slam into puddles of water as he makes his way down the fire break. Lush vegetation rises from either side of the trail. He follows Number Forty who is ahead in the distance.

Deep sand slows Cory's stride. He continues to wipe the water from his face. He can see his breath and his hands are red from the numbing cold. With only the sound of rain and his breathing for company, he runs silently and alone. Candidates run behind and in front of him, up the hills and down around the bends through the meadows.

He follows the marks of red tape streamers. With each stride, he lands carefully. He doesn't want to twist his ankle. Somewhere ahead, Billy is setting the pace. Cory thinks about the obstacle course and its sheer madness.

The evaluators are looking for something more than coordination. They are looking to see how the candidates deal with pain. For a week they have pushed them without mercy, perhaps too far.

Men are becoming ill. Wounds are becoming infected, and tempers are flaring. Throughout the daily formations, Cory watches the numbers of candidates diminish to one-hundred and seventy. Candidates quit in the night or become too sick or injured to go on. The men remaining are in it for the long haul.

Cory knows that everyone left just wants to finish the course. It's a personal challenge, something different for everyone; something no one has to understand, just respect. Broken feet, infected blisters, or sickness - these men ignore them all.

It's just an understanding. People will die trying to finish, if they must. It's a personal quest where physical trauma is not of any significance. There's something deeper at stake, something almost spiritual.

* * *

As a man's body starts to collapse, something else takes over. Something is driving these men past their physical limitations. Cory pictures his father in the public storage yard. He envisions his childhood and how his father always thought the worst of him. That's powerful enough to keep him going.

Germany is now a faint memory.

* * *

Cory crests the last hill and sees the finish line in the distance. His swollen ankles send dull pain up his legs, but he will not be stopped. He passes runners who wobble moving like exhausted zombies on the side of the road. Number Forty stumbles and falls and Cory steps out his stride, leaving them all behind.

* * *

Half way through their three weeks, Albert sits on the edge of his bunk. The day's events are complete. So far, the candidates have covered one hundred and twenty miles. Through the door, candidates step in from the darkness. Each candidate slowly limps to his bunk. The atmosphere is somber as each man licks his wounds.

Like a hospital ward, limping candidates wander from bunk to bunk. Cory is busy repacking his gear. Albert gingerly unties one of his boot laces. Painfully he removes the well-worn boot and sees a mangled and twisted sock soaked with blood.

He slowly peels it from his foot and flaps of skin tear off as he pulls. He bites his lower lip. With the sock removed, his eyes fill with tears of pain. The entire foot looks like it has been stripped of skin. Deep infected blisters surround the raw tissue. He groans.

"That's got to smart," Cory says tightening up a strap on his rucksack.

"Cory, what am I gonna do?"

Cory shrugs his shoulders. He has no good ideas for Albert's feet. His helping other people doesn't usually turn out so good.

Albert props his foot on top of his muddy boot, "This ruck is killing me. I can't walk anymore." Fear comes over him as he stares at his mangled foot. "You got to help me, McGuire!"

Cory looks into eyes of desperation for a moment. "I don't gotta do anything, Al!"

"Look at this man! Look at it. . ." he moans, tossing his bloody sock into the corner.

"I see it," Cory says. "But I have no idea what we can do that will make it any better."

"Really?" Albert asks him. "How bad is it? Is it as bad as it feels?"

Cory is careful not to show anything on his face. "It's not good, Al. It doesn't look good at all."

"That's all you got to say?" Albert says,

with tears still in his eyes.

"Yes."

Albert can't move, but he's mad. "For almost two weeks you've been parading around here like you're God's gift. I don't know why your feet ain't jacked up but look around."

"Why?"

"It's just not me, Cory. It's everybody. It's all of us!"

Cory looks around and he knows how bad everyone is hurting. But he can only help himself, so the rest can't really matter. He looks back at Albert but says nothing.

"I'm starting to wonder if you ain't got some magic formula."

"What are you talking about?"

"I'm talking about why you look so good. You always look squared away. Why is that?"

"I guess I just got something you guys don't." Cory pauses and moves close to Albert's face to lower his voice.

"You got to want it, Al. You got to want it more than anything in the world, and you got to have a reason to want it," he whispers.

Pain-filled tears roll down Albert's face. "I can't, man. My feet are done. Help me out."

"Al, I can't help you!" Cory snaps. "I've tried to help people all my life and where did it get me? Where did it get them? Nowhere, that's where! I'm here to get *me* through this. If I mess up then I pay, nobody else. You're here to get *you* through this. If you can't hang, quit! And get your sorry feet to the medic."

Before Albert can reply, a Green Beret walks through the door.

"All right. Listen up! First call has been changed from 0200 hours to 0600 hours. You're gonna get eight hours tonight. You better make good use of it and hit those racks. Lights out in fifteen minutes." He looks down toward his feet. "Somebody wipe this blood up off my floor. I might slip and kill myself."

After the sergeant turns and walks out, Cory grabs his bag and heads for the latrine. Inside he finds an empty stall. He

looks around to see if anyone is watching
and then closes the door behind him. He
sits on the toilet and unlaces his boots.
He pulls his bag near. He takes off his
first boot, then his second.

Sitting, he stares down and sees two
blood-soaked socks. He ignores the bile
rising in his stomach and quickly removes
his socks. He doesn't have the luxury of
emotions which don't help anyway.

His feet are bloody and swollen, looking
almost as bad as Albert's. An entire
toenail dangles freely off the side of his
big toe. Both heels look like chunks have
been carved from them and blisters the size
of silver dollars ooze thick dark fluid.
Opening his bag, he reaches in. He pulls
out a clean moist rag and scrubs his feet.
He uses some soap and wipes his feet clean,
all the while biting on the inside of his
cheek until he tastes blood. He puts on
another pair of socks and quickly pulls his
boots back on.

Standing up, he removes his shirt and
tries to blot the raw skin on the small of

his back and shoulders. The rucksack straps and padding have rubbed his back and skin to raw flesh. He puts his shirt back on and stuffs the blood-soaked rag back into his bag.

He hears a door open and someone slowly walks by. Looking underneath the stall walls, Cory sees boots. The man walks to the end and back again. Cory sees the boots stop in front of his stall. After a moment, the boots walk away and out the door. Cory gives a sigh of relief, collects his gear and leaves the latrine.

Outside, standing in the shadows, he hears, "You know what they say?"

He stops in his tracks. Trotten is standing in the dark, leaning against the wall. An eerie glow casts from his smoldering cigarette.

"They say that pain is nothing more than weakness escaping the body. Do you believe that?"

Cory says, "Yeah. I guess I do."

The first sergeant says, "Do, do, do. To do, to do, or not to do, what to do? I don't know, but I think circles are round, boxes are square, and you are who you are, no matter what the pain may say."

Cory looks out the side of his eye at him for a moment. Trotten, cigarette discarded, and hands cupped to his eyes, continues.

"I see many assorted soldiers in uniform. Some bigger. Some smaller. But they're all soldiers. And the thing is, they want me to see the difference."

He drops his hands and looks at Cory. "How can I see the difference? Maybe if I just use the same old, tired grading matrixes and stop watch, I'll learn everything I need to know. Somehow though, I don't think so."

Trotten holds a finger up. "I know. I'll throw away the stop watch and let you all show me who you are - really. Surely, I will see the differences then. You're bound to show me the real you eventually. I've got nothin' but time."

Trotten slowly backs away and out of sight until his words are hanging on the breeze. "We'll see who you really are. I

think we are both gonna be surprised.
Actually, Seventy-six, you're an open book-
and you don't even know it."

* * *

Back at the hut a few minutes later, Cory
packs his kit in silence.

"You get lost out there?" Albert asks.

"Nope."

"We get eight hours rack time tonight."

Cory doesn't reply.

"Cory, you all right?"

Cory thinks about that question. He
doesn't know the answer, but it doesn't
really matter.

"Just fine," he answers softly.

* * *

At exactly 0200-hours, explosions rock
the compound. Green Berets walk around the
huts tossing grenade simulators. In the
darkness, the candidates respond in chaos.

"Let's go, sleeping beauties. It's time
to go to work. Form it up outside. Let's
go!"

"I thought they were going to let us
sleep?" Albert groans.

"Change of plans, I guess," Cory says, picking up his gear and moving outside.

Albert sits on his bunk for a moment looking bewildered. He watches everyone walk by. He grabs his pillow and throws it against the wall. "Great."

Outside in the darkness, Cory's ears are still ringing from the simulators. Smoke swirls gently, rising up and away. Men move swiftly from every direction going to formation. Barely visible, Cory watches silhouettes move by. The air is cold and damp. He can feel it cutting right through him. He quickly puts his thirty-pound web belt with suspenders on. Canteens, butt pack, ammo pouches, and navigation equipment make up his personal gear.

In his right thigh pocket, a map is folded into a plastic zip bag. A compass hangs off his shoulder strap and is stuffed inside his fatigue shirt. He picks up the corners of his sixty-five-pound ruck at the frame. He lifts up and over the ruck sack and slides it down the other side of his back. With two quick tugs, he pulls the shoulder straps tight, careful not to wince with the pain. Making his way over to formation, he finds his place.

Down the row, Billy stands grinning. Number One-hundred, Albert, slowly and painfully limps to his place in formation behind Cory. To Cory's left and down a few men, he spots Number Ninety-eight. His rucksack hangs tightly packed and he wears his hat with the brim low over his eye brows. He stands poised and strong. Cory's impressed by the image he sees silhouetted in the darkness. He can sense his confidence and he respects that.

* * *

A figure walks in front of the formation as the men rock from side to side trying to stay warm.

"All right listen up! Rack time is over, and in the future, I suggest you get moving a lot faster." He raises his hand. "Who here really thought we were gonna let you guys sleep all night?" No one raises their hands. He pauses to look at the candidates. "We still got another week and you already look like casualties."

Indeed, the ranks of men are worn and beaten. The lack of sleep and food is taking its toll. The uniforms are torn and hastily sewn and patched. Like rag dolls, with sunken eyes and scratched faces, the candidates stand, though some just barely. They've covered hundreds of miles on foot. Over hills, through woods and streams, and across valleys, they have pushed themselves to beat the stop watch at every turn.

"There are one-hundred and forty-two of you left. At this rate, there will be no one left come next week."

* * *

The candidates are dropping like flies. Broken legs, concussions, heat exhaustion, hypothermia, and sickness plague many of the candidates. And even though many of them want to continue, their bodies are giving up on them. Like Albert, other men stand in the ranks with injuries that require attention.

Cory looks down at the boot of the man standing next to him. The man doesn't bother trying to lace it. A piece of duck tape is fastened around the top holding it together. His ankle is obviously broken. He stares ahead like a zombie.

"Tonight's mission is a ten-hour land navigation exercise. You must successfully navigate to four locations. At each point located you will be given a new set of coordinates. There will be no use of flashlights except to plot your routes on your map. You will talk to no one. This is not a team event. You must navigate as individuals. You will be spread out over sixty miles of terrain. If you should become a casualty, activate your starburst flare. Make sure it clears the trees, gentlemen, because you only have one. Stay at that location and we'll find you...eventually. Now, move out to your designated trucks."

* * *

Eight trucks crank up their cold diesel engines. Freezing wind whips through the Deuce and a Half's truck bed. The front canvass section is missing. Candidates huddle down close to their knees. Number Ninety-eight cracks a light stick in the darkness, the eerie green illuminating his face. Cory watches him, and then their eyes meet. Number Ninety-eight smirks.

After traveling an hour, the trucks come to a stop in some desolate location where two sand roads intersect amongst the heavy wood line. Cory jumps off and finds a spot on the ground to lay out his map. On his knees, he closely studies his map by red-lensed flash light. He places a finger at his current location, and with his other hand he runs a finger up the map to the location he believes to be his first navigation point.

Suddenly another candidate starts ranting and raving. "That's it! That is it!"

Cory just looks at him. The candidate continues.

"I can't take this anymore!" In the dark the candidate silhouette paces back and forth ripping up his map.

"Get me out of this frozen hell hole. You people are crazy! You're all out of your minds!"

A Green Beret approaches him and quietly walks him away. Cory turns off his flashlight and then stuffs his map into his shirt. He looks out into the night, seeing only ghostly shadows of his surroundings. He opens his compass, and fluorescent light shoots out. He takes a reading then looks down at his pace count beads and pushes them to the top of the string.

He takes off at a run disappearing into the darkness. After an hour or two traversing the sand roads and trails, underneath his breath, Cory counts out his pace.

"Seventy-five, Seventy-six, seventy-seven. . .six-hundred."

He stops, pulls another bead down and looks around. Pulling his map out and using the light from his compass to check his location, he points to an intersection on the map, then looks around.

Suddenly, he hears footsteps. A candidate comes into view from the opposite direction. Passing by, he stomps his boot down twice.

Cory watches him fade away, then takes off again.

Another two hundred meters, he counts, "Seventy-four, seventy-five, Seventy-six, seventy-seven. . .eight-hundred." He stops, and in the darkness, looks around, checking his map again.

Refolding it and stuffing it away, he mutters, "Too far. I'm too far." He battles down his frustration.

He lowers to a knee and takes some water from his canteen. Looking up, he sees the clouds part, revealing a bright moon. Then, he looks to his immediate right. As his eyes adjust, he sees an intersection slowly take shape.

"That's it. It's right there."

He puts his canteen away, points his compass, and takes off up the road.

The forest is closing in. The trail is narrow and uneven. Running, walking, breathing heavy, counting his pace, the narrowing trail turns him left and right. Cory walks slower, brushed by tree limbs and bushes until, finally, he's halted, unable to go any further. In the darkness, he stands, listening. He recognizes the sound of running water. Taking a few more steps, he feels his boots start to fill with water. Then a little further, although he cannot see it, he's halted by a fallen log. Trying to look from left to right, he imagines he's trapped, entangled in a densely-vegetated stream bed. He hears a distant and muffled flare being fired. He looks up, seeing a starburst souring off in the distance. He watches it, then with a sudden fear and determination, forces himself over the log, pulling vines off, battling to move forward.

He pulls out his map and compass. Cory slides his finger along the route until it stops where he thinks he's at. "This isn't here. This stream doesn't exist. Come on. Think. Ahead. It's got to be up ahead."

Cory puts his equipment away, and forces his way through, untangling as he goes. Further on, exhausted, Cory squeezes through a few more inches.

He stops, breathing hard. "I can't—I can't go—I just can't go—"

Taking a deep breath and holding it before letting it out, he hears a faint squelching sound close by. He lets out his breath and tries to breathe quieter. Then, he hears it.

Intermittent sounds of radio squelching ahead. Cory climbs up the side of the stream bed and looks. He sees the beam of a red flashlight moving through the trees.

"I can't believe it."

Cory moves like lightning toward the light and the turn-in point where an instructor waits.

* * *

Moving on to his next point and much colder now, Cory runs a road. Steam rises. He weaves back and forth, stumbling. The dirt road thins again, becoming uneven. He looks down at his wrist to check the time, forgetting his watch has been removed. He looks back up to the road ahead.

A shadowy candidate, running by in the opposite direction, says in a whisper,

"Point seventeen ain't out this way."

Cory continues to run never acknowledging him. He starts down a hill. It's rocky, uneven, and cut deep. At the bottom, he's narrowed to a small trail again. He runs around a few corners, and up ahead, sees something. He sees a candidate standing still, compass to cheek, taking a reading. His face glows green from the luminescence.

Cory walks toward him. Up close, the candidate turns and looks at Cory.

"I'm out of here. We're lost." He moves past Cory and heads in the direction where Cory had just been.

Cory watches him for a moment, then looks back down the trail. He can't see more than a few feet in front of him. He pulls his compass out and takes a reading. Then, he puts his hands on his knees, bending over to take the load off his back.

"Come on, think. Think, dang it. Go back. Go back where? Everyone's going back. Come on, think."

Boom! A starburst rockets through the trees back at the top of the hill where the last candidate is now. Cory watches it, noticing it light up the forest around him. He now sees the brightly lit trail in front of him. And something's there. On the trail, in the mud, a fresh set of foot prints can be seen ahead. Cory, getting down on his hands and knees, feels for the boot prints and checks for any coming back. There are none.

"Hmmm." He takes off down the trail. In the sky above, the starburst slowly fizzles out.

* * *

It's early morning, pre-dawn. Cory's exhausted, running and walking fast, counting, clicking down beads, taking readings with his compass as the sun begins to rise. It's gotten even colder. His hair, his runny nose, uniform—everything is frozen.

* * *

Down another dirt road, it's snowing hard, and Cory's walking slower. He pulls out his canteen, tilts it to his lips to find only a trickle coming out. He shakes it, hearing the block of ice knocking inside. Putting it away, he stops and looks to his front. He sees a wide, waist-deep river in front of him. Eerie sharp, bone-like branches stick out. Its name: "Bones Fork River."

Cory pulls out his map again, seeing the routes he's covered so far. He's drawn lines, going from the left side, across to the right. He puts the map away, looks down at his boots, then starts to cross, hoping for the best. The ice-cold brown water comes up to his waist. A wind comes up and the snow falls heavier like a blizzard. Slowly and carefully he reaches the other side and stops.

After a moment, something catches his attention. In all the stark white wilderness where nothing seems clear anymore, the scent of smoke fills his senses. He follows the smell and sees a slight billowing of black-gray rising through the trees.

Cory crashes through bushes and branches. His compass is out, guiding him. He stops, looks up, and sees a small fire and pick-up truck in the distance. He walks into the small camp. Four candidates sit under trees, frozen, exhausted, beaten, covering themselves with their green ponchos. They extend their boots out toward the small flame attempting to warm their feet. They all watch Cory as he passes by. He approaches the driver's window. An evaluator sits inside with the heat on. Cory knocks on the glass.

Without looking, the Green Beret rolls down the window a quarter of an inch. Cory takes the piece of paper he'd been given at his last point and slides it through the window. His hands shake from the cold. The Green Beret looks at it, then at his watch and after a moment, says, "Okay, Seventy-six. Move out over there with the rest of them." The window goes up.

Cory finds a tree and collapses on the ground. Snow falls, covering him like a pristine blanket.

CHAPTER ELEVEN

LAND NAVIGATION COURSE CAMP MACKALL - DAY

A few hours later, Cory, Number Ninety-eight, and a few other candidates are in the back of a canvas-covered truck as it continues to snow. Cory and Number Ninety-eight sit across from each other, closest to the front cab section. The vehicle starts to pull away, then, suddenly, stops.

An instructor from the front shouts back to them. "Make room for one more back there."

Hearing footsteps slowly come around to the back of the truck, Cory and the others see Albert emerge. He's frozen and shaking violently. He tries to speak, but his words are nothing more than unintelligible mumbles.

One of the candidates mutters, "Wow."

Albert grabs the top of the tailgate and tries to climb in. The candidates closest to him inside the truck pull him aboard. He lies on the floor, still shaking, trying to speak. The candidates start wrapping him up to get him warmer.

Albert finally manages to say, "Cory…I—I knew—you'd make it." Albert looks over at Cory with a slight smile, as the truck begins to pull away again. "No—no—heat stroke-today."

Cory looks at Albert for a moment, his heart breaking for his pain. His father's face flashes through his mind as a reminder, though; mind your own business and no one gets hurt.

After an awkward silence, he replies, "That's good, Al." He looks away, unable to look at Albert again. Maybe it's the fatigue but he almost feels like crying for himself, for his father and for them all.

Albert looks down at his feet and

stammers, "I—I can't feel—any—thing."

Cory shakes his head and moves toward him. He gets down on his hands and knees and reaches his own frozen fingers toward Albert's laces. He knows what he'll find. He glances up and catches Albert's tear-filled eyes. He's rocked by the memory of his father's eyes. He just stares, unable to get a grip.

After a moment, another candidate speaks up and moves Cory gently away.

"That's okay, buddy, we got ya. Let's get you on the seat and get those boots off."

Cory takes his seat and wills his stomach to calm down. This is no place for being too involved. He watches the other men work on Albert's boots and steels himself.

"Oh man! That's bad," says one of them.

Cory closes his eyes, knowing what they see. A candidate yanks the other boot and sock off, gasping at Albert's frozen, swollen, and bloody feet. They go to work, putting his feet under their shirts, up against their bellies.

"We got to get his feet warmed up," one

of the men states.

Another says, "Pull some gauze wrap out of my ruck for these blisters. They're infected bad."

Cory can feel Albert's hound dog gaze, but he stays focused looking at the floor and his own feet. He's glad it's dark because he feels his own eyes welling up.

He turns away as Albert whispers, "Cory? Cory? You all right, man?"

* * *

It's a new day. The land navigation exercise is over and somehow, he and Albert survived. And back at the SFAS facility, a new phase of evaluation has begun.

Looking up at a loud speaker on a pole, Cory hears the "Chordettes" 1954 recording.

"Mr. Sandman, bring me a dream, make him the cutest that I've ever seen..."

Sitting on the ground while eating an MRE with Number Ninety-eight, he says, "What's that all about?"

The candidate casually looks up and tells him, "Looks like team week's begun."

"What's that mean?" Cory asks, not sure

he wants to know.

"About a hundred and fifty miles of team endurance events."

Cory nods and thinks on that for a moment. "Why the song?"

"What? Mr. Sandman?" Number Ninety-eight says with a grin. "Ol' Mr. Sandman. Why he's the first event."

With all he's already been through in SFAS, he's not sure he'll be able to survive being on a team. Relying on others is not his strong suit. He can feel Number Ninety-eight's eyes on him, but he can't meet that gaze. He can't risk the observant candidate seeing the fear in his eyes.

* * *

In the rain with a duffel bag full of sand lashed in the center of four iron poles which criss-cross like a tic tac toe board, Cory's small team heaves the contraption.

Cory, Billy, Albert, and another candidate pick up their ends and place the pole behind their necks, so it rides on their rucksacks. The obvious strain and pain can be seen in their faces. Cory and Billy lead from the front left and right. Evaluators stand nearby, watching the team.

One of them asks the other, "How much does that thing weigh?"

"Not including those poles, their individual rucksacks, and equipment, I'd say about four-hundred pounds. Only ten miles, though."

The men laugh. Then the new man asks, "What's next?"

"Ammo crate carry. Another ten miles."

Cory and his team keep moving forward so focused on their heavy and torturous assignment that they forget about the evaluators following and evaluating them.

It's been hours and they continue to walk. Cory, with head lowered and rain pouring off his face, struggles with each step. Each step feels like the last he can bear.

Billy's exhaustion is evident and so is Albert's. The fourth man has stumbled several times, but no one speaks a word.

A helicopter flies low overhead and as

one unit, they all glance up. A red and white medical cross is painted across its belly. It moves over the trees, out of sight.

Cory's team walks up a steep, sandy hill with a Green Beret evaluator following them. In sheer pain and torture, they make the grade.

Albert shakes his head and says, "Looks like someone else bit the dust. That isn't exactly encouraging."

Billy tries to lighten the mood by answering, "You ever just wake up some mornings feeling like a pack mule?"

Cory doesn't even have the energy to talk, let alone joke. He wants to stay focused on the mission. "Come on. Let's get this thing done already."

Ignoring Cory's short command, Billy glances back over his shoulder at the rear members of the team.

"How you holding up back there, Zullini?"

Albert, doing his best to keep up, says, "One foot in front of the other, right?"

"That boy has got a lot of heart," Billy

says to Cory hoping to change Cory's attitude toward Albert.

Almost to himself, Cory mutters, "And it won't ever be enough."

They crest the top of the hill and Cory sees a road that goes on forever. "Let's go. We're almost home," he says as he tries for some motivational encouragement.

The evaluators follow behind them, recording actions, behaviors and conversations.

* * *

The sun is almost down, and twelve exhausted candidates are walking by two's, struggling with yet another seemingly superhuman test.

Cory and Albert shuffle quickly and painfully with a long narrow ammo crate held between them. The cold, relentless rain has stopped.

The skin's been rubbed clear off their wrists from the heavy load on the rope handles, and their useless hands are curled upward to keep the handles from sliding down.

Albert is barely able to hang on. His handle starts to slide down, forcing his wrist to straighten. "I'm losing it! I'm losing it!" he cries to the team.

Angrily, Cory screams, "Don't you drop it! Don't you do it!"

Albert in even greater distress yells, "I can't hang on! It's slipping!"

Cory, always annoyed with Albert's insufficiencies yells back, "Come on! Don't you quit on me! Pick it up! We're running out of time!"

Albert admits defeat, saying, "Let it down! Let it down!"

Cory screams, No!" Then it dawns on him there's an alternative to failure in their grasp and he calls out, "Switch!"

Everyone stops, softly setting down the crates which are filled with simulated explosives.

Cory and Albert quickly switch sides, pick up the heavy crate and move out again and regain speed and distance.

From a near distance, a Green Beret watches them slowly approach his location.

Exhausted, the team carries the crates with both hands now, dragging themselves along.

Cory and Albert make their way in silence. Billy, with the other candidate, is doing the same, as they move beyond the Green Beret evaluators.

Finally, the evaluator says, "Put 'em down."

Billy's team puts the crate down and both men collapse beside it.

Cory and Albert painfully lower their crate, too. Cory remains standing as Albert collapses on the ground.

Albert looks at his wrists, touching the deep wounds. Cory just looks at him. Billy, back on his feet, passes by Cory, looks at Albert and gives him a wink.

Then he says to Cory, "Yes sir. A lot of heart."

Cory gives a slight nod, albeit, a reluctant one.

* * *

The long day and night of moving forward in extreme pain is over. For Cory, operating within the team framework has been almost as painful as the physical part of it. He can do the physical stuff and when it's over, it's over. He was raised to be tough. Much like his father's tirades, when they were over, they were over, and he'd survived them all, somehow.

But also, like those fear-filled childhood days, there are the unknowns. He prefers his lone wolf style. A team with a weak link will kill the whole team. He shakes his head.

Back at the SFAS facility, utterly exhausted, Cory grabs his shower kit first thing and makes his way to the latrine.

He's sitting on the toilet seat in a private stall. His back's been rubbed raw. He's staring down at his feet, almost too tired to move. Finally, he grabs a bottle of NU-SKIN from his laundry bag. The front label reads, "*NU-SKIN for minor blister irritation.*"

So, desperate for some relief from the pain he doesn't let people see, he understands all too well the warning on the back label about not using it on open wounds.

He opens the bottle. After a moment, he looks down at his feet which look far worse than a few days ago. Swollen, discolored, infected blisters cover most of his feet. It's this or gangrenes at this rate.

His feet are in a small tub. Cory leans over the tub, hesitates, glances around to check that he's still alone in the latrine, then stuffs a clean sock in his mouth to bite down on. He quickly pours the liquid over his feet.

The instantaneous and excruciating pain slams his back into the toilet tank and he sucks in air through his nose. The sock muffles his screams of anguish and his tears run freely down his face. Quaking from the pain, he grips the toilet paper dispenser which would have been crushed had it not been metal.

Somehow, he's kept his feet in the small tub and after another long moment, the pain subsides, and Cory stares at the back of the stall door, groaning deeply. He pulls the sock out of his mouth and lays it over his knee.

He wonders if the cadre has noticed his behavior. Has he shown any sign of weakness? He almost chuckles. He probably has. How often had his father told him what a disappointment he was?

He's too tired to retrace his steps. Their time at Mackall is almost complete and he's done his best. Will it be good enough? He'll find out on graduation day. Like so many other things in his life, he can't do any more to affect the outcome.

He pulls his feet out of the tub and gently pats them to be sure they're dry. He wraps them the best he can with the gauze he has left and then pulls on clean socks.

This time Trotten and his telltale cigarette are nowhere to be seen when he leaves the latrine.

CHAPTER TWELVE

TROOP HUT CAMP MACKALL - EARLY EVENING

In the hospital-like ward, Cory busily repacks some equipment. The door opens, and a Green Beret enters.

"Where's Seventy-six?"

Cory looks up. "Here, Sergeant."

"Master Sergeant Trotten needs to see you right now in his office."

"Yes, Sergeant." Cory moves past the Green Beret and out into the quad. His heart is beating fast, but he keeps his pace deliberate and even. His summons can't mean anything good.

At Trotten's office, Cory gives the door

a good solid rap, then waits for an acknowledgement.

"Come in, Seventy-six." Trotten sits behind his desk and a Green Beret is seated in the corner.

Cory steps inside and closes the door behind him.

Trotten nods at Cory. "Have a seat, McGuire."

Cory's nervous as he moves to a chair in front of Trotten and sits down but he keeps his jaw set and chin high. Seeing the Green Beret sitting in the corner, he wonders if he's being cut from Selection.

Trotten looks steadily at Cory, then looks at the Green Beret. He looks at Cory again and after a moment says, "Let me just start out by saying, McGuire, that I'm deeply, deeply sorry."

Everything is running through Cory's head. Has he given too much away? Have they seen too much of the real him - soft and scared? Too selfish? Not selfish enough? It could be all or any of those things. He battles to keep his fear off his face.

What had the evaluators written him up for and he never even realized? Was he caught sleeping? Out of uniform? Had he looked at someone the wrong way? Or was it that he's not fast enough or smart enough for the Special Forces? He can't speak, so he sits waiting for the axe to fall.

Trotten clears his throat, then continues.

"At 1700-hours this evening. . ."

Cory raises his chin a bit higher and meets Trotten's gaze. *Here it comes.*

"Your Father, Robert C. McGuire, was involved in a fatal accident."

No, no, no! With surreal clarity, Cory knows and understands everything. All the times he's feared this exact moment flash into his mind like a distorted collage. His eyes begin to fill with tears.

Trotten lowers his voice and leans forward, a yellow slip of paper in his hand. "I'm sorry, son. The phone call that we received said that he probably died instantly; there was no suffering whatsoever." Trotten sets down the message

145

and looks at Cory.

After a moment, Cory slowly rises from his chair and turns away from the desk. Facing the wall, he forces out the question first on his mind.

"Did he hurt anyone else?"

"No. No one else was involved," Trotten says.

Cory clears his throat. "Did they say where it happened? Do you know what happened? When?"

"Says here, Detroit. On the railroad tracks near a public storage yard. They identified him by the wallet in his pocket. The train couldn't stop in time to avoid him. I'm very sorry."

Before he can stop it, a gasp escapes his mouth. Cory shakes his head, partly in disbelief. Nothing he'd done has made any difference. Not the money, not finding him a home, not going into the same Army that his father had so idolized.

Keeping his voice even, Trotten speaks to Cory's back, much like a father might speak to a son in pain.

"I know you're going to want to leave tomorrow and of course, you need to do that. We'll have a car ready to take you out whenever you're ready."

Cory turns around, looks at the Green Beret, then at Trotten. He starts backing out of the room, forcing away tears.

"Yeah. I need to go. My sister won't. . .," he begins. He shakes his head as if to clear it. "I'll start packing my gear."

He walks out the door and closes it behind him. As he walks away, Trotten comes after him.

"McGuire!"

Cory turns around, swiping his eyes on his shirt sleeve. Trotten approaches, then stops when they are two feet apart.

"Do you know this is the last night of SFAS? This is it. It's over. Finished. We can't arrange transport until tomorrow anyway. You've pounded out three-hundred and eighty some-odd miles here. A twenty-eight-mile ruck march, and you can say that you at least finished."

Cory feels defeated. His father has won.

How could he have ever fooled himself by thinking it would turn out any other way? But a train?

He looks at the floor and shakes his head, shoulders slumped. "I know. But it just doesn't matter anymore. I don't wanna finish." Cory turns and starts walking away.

Trotten calls after him. "You can't quit, McGuire!"

Cory stops. With tears in his eyes he turns back abruptly and retraces his steps until he's in Trotten's face.

"No. I get to quit. I. Get. To. Quit! I've never been allowed to give up on anybody or anything in my entire life. I've *had* to be there. No matter how much it hurt. I had to be there. Even when I knew nothin' was gonna change, I was there. I'm *always* there."

Cory pauses for a moment, takes a raspy breath as though he's been running, then continues. "For the first time in my life, I thought, I *really* thought, I wanted something for me. For me! Now I know I was just running – trying to prove that I was better than *him* – better than a has-been drunk who hurt people all the time. That I could make it. I could be somebody." Cory laughs, but it's harsh, almost a sob.

"Can't quit? Do you know that I waited up every night for him? That I worried about him? That I cared? Night and day. Did you know that? I stayed awake so he didn't burn the house down with his cigarettes. Did you know that every siren that went by my window, I thought it was for my dad? Do you know what that's like? Do you!? Nothing I did worked. I couldn't save him when I was with him, and I couldn't save him now. You say you know me. You say I'm opened wide for all the world to see. Well, guess what? Now you see me, don't you? Pathetic tears and all. Pain and all. Rage and all. I really don't care. I could honestly care less about *anyone*, especially now. So, consider it a favor that I'm leaving because I don't belong here. I don't belong here at all." Cory's standing straight now, almost daring Trotten to say something. His hands are fisted as though he's ready for a fight.

Trotten looks for a long minute into Cory's eyes, then pulls his beret out of his leg pocket. He places it on his head.

"We're not so different, you and I, Cory. We're not so different at all. And I know what I see. And I do know who and what you are. I know what's inside you and I know it's all right. You didn't come here to prove to your father or anyone else that you could be better than him. You came because you want to be here, so you could be part of a team. Be there, Seventy-six. Be at that start line tonight at zero-hundred hours. Be there, not to prove anything to your father, but be there because that's who you are. And be there because it still burns inside you to go the distance."

Cory looks at the ground and then says quietly, "I'm sorry. I just can't."

Cory walks away and around the corner drops to his knees, hands clenched. Weeping like a man whose heart has been torn in two, he cries, "Why'd you do it to me? Why, Dad? How could you do it? Even now you're killing me. There's nothing else I can do for you. Please stop."

CHAPTER THIRTEEN

TRAINING GROUND CAMP MACKALL - NIGHT

Hours pass and the SFAS grounds are dark and quiet. Everything is calm except for the dark silhouettes which can be seen moving slowly to the other side of the small base.

Before long, all the candidates are gathered at the final event starting position. Trotten stands in front and starts to issue instructions.

"Follow the green chem lights which are placed at one-hundred-meter intervals. There is no set time limit. If you finish, you're doing well. Eight hours is not unheard of. Just do your best, gentlemen."

Billy approaches Albert as Trotten continues and says, "Where's Cory?"

Albert looks around. "I don't know. The last time I saw him he got called into the office."

Billy looks at Albert. "Did he get pulled?"

"I'm not sure."

Billy looks back at the edge of the base fence. "Well, he just better hurry and get out here."

* * *

Trotten looks out into the faces of the candidates, looking for Cory. He looks down at his watch and back out into the candidate faces one more time. Finally, he holds up his stopwatch, clicks it and gives the command.

"Move out!"

The candidates start moving down the road. Trotten watches them all pass by. Then, out of nowhere, running from a distance out of the dark, in full gear, runs Cory. He reaches the start position and passes right by Trotten.

A Green Beret standing next to him with a clip board says, "What's with this guy?"

Trotten smiles and follows Cory with his eyes. "I know what's with this guy."

The Green Beret points his pen in Cory's direction and says, "That's not-"

Trotten interrupts. "It sure is."

* * *

Cory leaves Trotten and the start position fading into the dark. He runs hard, passing candidates left and right. Finally, toward the front, he passes Billy.

Over his shoulder, he hollers, "You comin' or what?"

Billy grins and says, "All right, McGuire! Now we got us a race!"

At mile eight Cory runs through a small stream and Billy follows close behind. At mile fifteen, on a long stretch, green chem lights mark the way, Cory in first and Billy twenty feet behind as they run.

Around mile twenty-two, Cory and Billy walk fast, side by side, up a hill. They move quietly up a section of old asphalt road and then over an old wooden bridge.

They continue going and going, seemingly forever, but their pace has changed. Cory's focused like always, but the fury is gone. He's glad for Billy's quiet company.

Making another mile, they now walk side by side. There is still no talking. The only sound is that of their boots hitting the ground and the swaying of their heavy rucks.

The chem lights seem to go on forever. Finally, as they round a corner, they see two Green Beret medics standing outside a truck.

"What's your name?" they yell in unison.

Cory, sweating profusely answers, "McGuire!"

"Where are you from?"

"Michigan!" Cory shouts.

Billy runs by.

The Green Beret shouts, "What's your name?"

Billy yells, "Johnson!"

"Where are you from?"

Billy grins, "Alabama!"

They leave the instructors watching until

they're out of sight.

CHAPTER FOURTEEN

LONG DISTANCE MARCH - CROSS COUNTRY - NIGHT

A helicopter flies by, swooping low overhead. Cory watches it for a moment then continues to walk with Billy who's falling back.

Cory's drenched with sweat, weaving back and forth like a drunken soldier. He stumbles, then starts to run. Further along his head hangs low. Breathing hard he staggers both left and right, his motor skills diminished, fluids dripping from both his nose and mouth. He tries to wipe it and misses, wiping his cheek instead.

He looks up to see, like double vision, a mirage-like assortment of green chem lights dancing around. He's exhausted and his reserves are spent. The road loses shape and then comes back. He hallucinates, seeing shadows running across the road, faces in the forest, green chem lights dripping eerie streams of fluorescent green fluid down trees into puddles on the road.

He hears voices laughing and screaming. Finally, Cory stumbles, collapses into the dirt. He struggles mightily to get back up, wobbling. He looks back and sees Billy weaving as well.

Cory's lost track of all time and place, willing himself to keep moving forward just as he can hear Billy refusing to quit not far behind him.

On another seemingly endless stretch of dirt road, Cory shuffles, runs, and walks, almost unable to lift his feet. He goes a few more steps. Then a few more. One more.

He drops to his knees and looks staring straight ahead.

"Rosssterrr Nummmberr Seven—ty-six."

In front of him is a Green Beret evaluator. Looking down at his stopwatch

and clip board he says matter-of-factly,
"Time, Seventy-six: five hours, twenty
minutes. Good job."

CHAPTER FIFTEEN

CLASSROOM CAMP MACKALL - DAY

In a classroom, eighty-five candidates are standing exhausted and at Attention.

The twenty-eight-mile plus road march ended a few hours ago. Cory, Billy, Albert, and Number Ninety-eight are among those remaining. Moving to the front, Trotten is followed by a few Green Berets. One of them hands him a piece of paper. There is silence as he unfolds and reads it.

"Those of you standing in this room are among the few that can say they have completed this evaluation. You have all done a fine job and that's something to be proud of." He looks at the men and allows a

full minute for his comment to sink into
their exhausted minds.

"Evaluators! Move to the front now."

Five Green Berets move to the front with
Trotten. Number Ninety-eight is among that
five. He passes by Cory, giving him a
penetrating look.

Trotten continues. "These five men have
been placed among your ranks at various
times. They are all Green Berets sent to
evaluate you from within."

Cory locks eyes with Number Ninety-eight
for a moment. *Well, I'll be.*

Trotten resumes. "If I call off your
roster number, please, quietly leave the
room. Those numbers are: 129—281—15—74—32—
003—68—261—103—44—78—009—10—222—101—001—75—
212—105—and—77."

Slowly candidates to the left and right
turn and walk out. Cory, Billy, and Albert
are left in the ranks that remain in the
room standing with several feet between
them.

Sixty candidates remain when the last
candidate leaves the room closing the door

behind him. Folding the piece of paper, Trotten tucks it into his pocket.

"Welcome to Special Forces school, gentlemen."

Number Ninety-eight smiles at Cory and the room breaks into a quiet, tired celebration as the remaining candidates realize they were the group chosen to continue.

Trotten quiets the men. "Your training is just beginning, and over the next several months you will be tested in many ways. The hard truth is, out of the sixty of you in this room, maybe, and I mean maybe, some of you might graduate with that class. And those who do will eventually be assigned to Special Forces A-teams. Just like the song says, 'One hundred men we'll test today, but only three win the Green Beret.' Good luck, men."

Cory turns and starts to head for the door. Trotten approaches him.

"McGuire, when you get things at home squared away, I expect to see you back here. You got a lot of training to do."

Cory looks Trotten in the eye and allows a weary but heartfelt smile. "I'll be back." And then, looking down at his boots, he says, "Besides, I just got these boots broke in."

Trotten roars as though this is the funniest thing he's heard in forever. For a moment, he rests his hand on Cory's shoulder.

"There's a vehicle outside waiting to take you back to Bragg. Go take care of business. *All* of it."

Cory looks at him, then at the classroom of the few candidates remaining. He's done here and it's time to go home. This time he doesn't expect his father to pick him up at the airport. In a way, there's a peace in that.

Cory walks out the door and sees the dark sedan waiting for him. On the pole, the loud speaker starts playing. It's "The Balled of the Green Beret" by Barry Sadler.

Cory stands and listens for a long moment, then picks up his gear, gets in the car and they drive away.

Don R. Kabrich

FADE TO BLACK

CHAPTER SIXTEEN

11 MONTHS LATER — AIR BASE, SAUDI ARABIA

"The day of reckoning is upon us, Parker. We can't wait any longer," says Colonel Davis, as they stride through the flight lines.

Parker, Cory's team leader, is a young officer but sharp minded and a careful listener. "Yes, Sir."

"We need that intel and we need it right now. Cloud cover! You'd think we'd built a satellite by now to see through this soup," Davis grumbles.

"I understand the urgency, Sir."

Davis glances at him. "I know you do. Is your team ready to go?"

"Yes, Sir. We've been ready for two weeks."

Davis snorts in frustration. "Those people in Washington don't know a good thing when they see it. All right. Better late than never. I just hope it's not too late. Where's your team room?"

Parker points ahead and to the right. "We've got a make shift isolation facility just this side of the hanger, Sir."

"Good. What have they been doing to keep themselves occupied?" Davis asks.

Parker laughs a little. "Besides going a little stir crazy, Sir? Just a little serious cross-training here and there."

Davis grins at Parker, then says, "Do I want to know what kind of cross training, Parker?"

Parker avoids eye contact as they continue to walk toward the front door.

* * *

Inside the isolation building with its blacked-out windows and bright artificial lighting, Billy is bent over, quickly disassembling and assembling an assault rifle on a table, instructing a class. He gives the class in a classic "over the top" form, mocking the cadre he once studied under back at Bragg.

"As a Weapons Sergeant, it's imperative that I be intimately familiar with all weapons foreign and domestic..."

On the table, he quickly takes different pieces apart. Continuing, he says, "Particularly, this here M-16. Well, it's mostly an M-16. We've also got some AK47 and M249 parts mixed in here. Although it may not be my first choice in a weapon, I might find myself in a situation that requires me to use it. And you should be familiar with it, too. There are many moving parts here that need be disassembled and assembled..."

Now Billy puts the mismatched pieces back together. "It's easy to get them mixed up. And if you find yourselves not afforded the luxury of light, you had better know how to work on this baby blind folded. Time!" Billy holds his hands up like he's just completed a hog tie.

Another team member calls out, "One minute twenty-four seconds."

Billy turns with the assembled weapon, pulls the bolt to the rear, and snaps it on safe. He's blind folded and smiling. He wears a new Special Forces insignia on his shoulder.

"Any questions?"

Billy's new team surrounds the table. Everyone is in desert fatigues laughing and whistling.

* * *

A little later, it's Cory's turn. He writes a complicated equation on the chalkboard as he lectures. Just below his feet, a long piece of green time fuse slowly burns. As he continues to write on the chalkboard he jokes with the team.

"There is a distinct difference between time fuse and demo cord. As an Engineer Demo Sergeant, I have been trained to know the difference. I am here to teach you the difference. Both look similar. However, time-fuse is made from black powder and has an R.E. factor of .45." He writes the number down and circles it.

"Whereas demo cord uses an explosive component called PETN which has an R.E. factor of 1.66." He writes this number down too and circles it.

"If you should mistakenly tie in a mix of demo cord, confusing it for time fuse, you will be in for a big, big surprise. Because it's more powerful than, say C-4 for example, a strand run from the East coast of the United States to the West coast will burn at approximately twenty-five-thousand-feet per second. That means about fifteen minutes coast to coast.

"Now, to calculate for time fuse, follow these simple rules." He looks up to be sure everyone's listening.

"First. Test burn a three-foot section of time fuse. Divide the time by three which equals burn time per one foot. The desired burn time should be multiplied by sixty. Then divide by the average burn time here. After that, multiply these numbers here behind the decimal by twelve for inches. Multiply these numbers over here behind this decimal by sixteen for the one sixteenth which will give you inches. Without the proper training, it will be difficult to time your fuse accurately."

Cory looks down at his watch, counting, "Five, four, three, two, one."

The time fuse fizzles out at precisely the right time. He turns to his amused team, his Special Forces insignia on his shoulder, and says, "Thus, your five-minute time fuse. Any questions?"

The team mates laugh and applaud. Cory takes a deep bow.

* * *

Colonel Davis and Captain Parker turn a corner and walk through the door. In front of them, an M.P. stands guard at another door which reads *AUTHORIZED PERSONNEL ONLY*.

They hold out their passes. The M.P. opens the door and they continue through to where Cory's erasing the chalkboard.

The team stops laughing when they see the two officers enter. Maps, charts, and equipment are spread about. Upon seeing Parker and Davis, Albert takes off his headset, sitting entrenched in a virtual mountain of communications equipment.

Davis looks around and says, "Hello, men. I trust you're ready to rock and roll."

The team slowly disperses and goes about their business quiet and reserved. Master Sergeant Gifford, the team sergeant, early forties, rough, tan and stocky, remains seated.

Spitting tobacco in a cup first, he says, "We're always ready, Sir."

Frustrated with the attitude, but understanding it, Davis says, "I know that, Gifford, and I want to personally apologize for the delay. I want to get you out there where you belong."

Gifford nods. "No need to apologize, Sir. I realize Washington has their head up their you-know-where."

In the background, Captain Parker closes his eyes and shakes his head.

Laughing, Davis says, "I would have to say you are one hundred percent correct in that assessment, Sergeant Gifford. But just remember, no matter how tame that lion may seem, people aren't willing to open that cage to find out. To tell you quite frankly, you boys scare the livin' heck out of Washington."

Gifford continues with a slight smile on his face. "Well, maybe you can pass the word on for me, Sir. There ain't no reason to be scared. We just want to do our job."

"And that you will, Gifford."

Gifford raises a brow in Parker's direction.

"Colonel Davis here just came from the TOC. We got a 'Go' status," Says Parker.

The team's ears suddenly perk up. Everyone's eyes meet. After a short pause, Davis says, "That's right. You got the green light on this one. Anyway, I just came by to pass the word along with your Team Leader here."

Davis turns and starts walking toward the door. "Intel's gonna be coming by to give you the final brief."

"When should we expect deployment, Sir?" Gifford asks.

Davis turns back and says, "Soon. Very,

very soon."

With that final word, Davis walks out the door. Gifford and Parker stare at each other, the team stares at them and then Parker shrugs his shoulders.

Gifford stands up, looks around and says, "You heard the man! Let's get it on!"

The team starts moving like lightning. Gifford looks over at a map. At the top, it reads *IRAQ*. There's a clear plastic overlay with plots, thumb tacks, and a greased pencil section in the middle which reads: *MOBILE SCUD SIGHT*.

CHAPTER SEVENTEEN

ISOLATION FACILITY - NIGHT

The team prepares to roll out and the isolation room must be cleared. The room glows red as a team member tears down the map and rolls it up. He's in full combat uniform with tiger stripe camouflage paint on his face.

The men move in quiet, efficient patterns. They sterilize the room, take down every map, chart, and note, load ammo in magazines, try on rucksacks, function check M-16s, test radios and test night vision devices.

Gifford and Parker get ready as well, quizzing the team as they go. Gifford, to

Cory, asks, "Name?"

"Mikey."

"Exfil?"

"Two zero niner three. Four eight five niner!"

Gifford points to himself now. "Blood type?"

Cory chirps, "O positive!"

Then Parker says to Billy, "Smoke?"

"Green!"

"Infil?"

"One eight three six. Two five zero two!"

Then Gifford snaps quickly to Albert. "What's my name?"

Albert says, "Mickey!"

"Go to hell plan?"

"Two-thousand meters, one-four-eight degrees from exfil!"

"M-203 grenade launchers?"

"Mikey, Marks, and Mighty!"

The quizzing continues randomly throughout the team as they continue to hustle about.

"Time check!"

"Eighteen twenty hours."

"Three hours four zero mikes."

"Roger that!"

"We're on it! We're on it!"

They continue checking, organizing, and walking back and forth. A rucksack gets hooked to a hanging scale which reads *155 LBS.*

* * *

The tailgate of the C-130 lowers as if in slow motion. The team staggers at the ready like shadowy astronauts.

A moon lit blanket of cloud cover sits just below them. Cory breathes into his oxygen mask, then Billy, then Albert.

A green light comes on and Gifford waves an arm. By ones and twos they walk forward, leaping out into the night. The team descends in a formation, one behind the other.

Cory races toward the clouds below, slamming in and through, then checks his altimeter. It reads *14,000 Ft.* He pulls his rip cord and sees his chute start to flutter open.

Just below the cloud cover, the team's

chutes start opening one by one. High above the desert floor they fly their square chutes.

Two fighter jets flying below radar scream below the team and bank right. In a moment, explosions light up the sky.

Cory checks his watch. It reads *0100 HRS*.

* * *

The team flies stealthily by parachute for a few kilometers, then start landing silently, one by one, forming a small circle on the desert floor. Cory lands on his feet, goes to a prone position on the ground, and aims his weapon down range.

Gifford, Parker, Billy, and Albert do the same. They wait, watching and listening. Far off they can hear intermittent explosions. Cory looks at Gifford who points at his watch and holds up two fingers. Cory looks down at his watch that reads *0145*.

At *0200*, Cory slips sand bags over his boots and ties them. A couple of team members kneel, facing out to keep watch. A few more cover the tracks left behind where they landed. Gifford gives the signal to move out. Everyone rises at the same time and takes up their positions. They move in a backwards V formation, spread apart, moving silently.

After moving through the desert a few kilometers, the point man suddenly stops and raises his fist. He hears or sees something ahead. The team freezes in place. The point man slowly kneels. The rest of the team does the same, training their weapons on assigned sectors. Finally, a small bird flutters away.

The point man gives the signal to move out again. Cory, Billy, and Albert rise moving forward. Gifford, in the middle of the wedge formation, makes eye contact with Cory. Using his hand, he double taps the side of his boot. Cory looks down at his pace count beads and holds up eight fingers.

Gifford nods, circles a finger overhead and points down at a passing location, the enroute rendezvous. Cory nods, repeats the motion, pointing as he passes for Billy to see.

Billy repeats the motion for Albert. Then Albert passes it along to the next team member and the team slowly fades into the landscape.

* * *

Looking through night vision goggles, Cory watches Parker confirm their location on the map. He then looks beyond the Captain's shoulder and sees the shadowy silhouette of a scud missile sight off in the distance. Parker kneels and takes off his own night vision goggles, looks at Gifford, then points to the location and gives a thumbs-up. Gifford nods, looks at the team, and then signals the team to split up.

The two elements move in opposite directions toward the scud missile site. Now at the edge of the outer perimeter, low crawling on his back, Cory cuts a barbed wire fence and crawls under and into the small compound. Inside he takes up a position for cover and waves the others in.

A large storage tank blocks his view of

the compound. The others come through and spread out. The team's eyes are on Gifford as he gives the signal to move out. He points at Cory.

Cory gives him a nod in return. Gifford and the others move while Cory stays behind.

Cory pulls out a claymore mine. He crawls back to the fence and sets it up. It's placed so it will blast toward the center of the compound and reads *FRONT TOWARD ENEMY*. He pulls out a trip wire and, several feet back, runs it low to the ground parallel to the fence. He attaches the wire to the claymore and activates the explosive device.

Cory moves to the edge of the storage tank, skirts around the side, and moves in. As he gets to the team's position, he sees Gifford staring up at something in the center of the compound. Cory moves over to his location.

"Exfil point secure," he whispers.

Still looking up, Gifford says, as if talking to himself, "I don't believe it. I just can't believe it."

Cory's internal alarm system kicks in. "What is it?" he snaps.

Gifford says in disbelief, "It's an oil well. We're sitting on a deserted oil well!"

Cory looks up at what Gifford's looking at. In the darkness, everything suddenly comes into focus. An oil rig stands in the center of the compound with various processing equipment scattered about. The compound's old, rusty, and long been deserted.

Parker's split team, like well-spaced shadows, slowly approach from the other side. Parker offers the challenge word. "Range wood."

Gifford confirms. "We're secure," he says.

"Roger that," Parker replies. "What do you think?"

Gifford shakes his head. "I'm convinced this is clearly not an active scud site."

Billy chimes in, "There ain't nothin' out here."

"What's going on, Sir?" Albert asks in a whisper.

Before Parker can answer, Gifford says, "I have a funny feeling it has something to do with that lion's cage."

CHAPTER EIGHTEEN

DESERT OIL RIG - NIGHT

The team makes final preparation and gets ready to move out. Gifford gives the command.

"We're out of here." Then he looks at Albert. "Alternate point man, shoot us an azimuth out of here."

Albert trots off saying, "I'm on it."

Cory's busy strapping down his ruck when Albert moves quickly behind him and heads for the barbed wire fence opening.

After a moment of silence, Billy says, "Man, we got burned."

Cory, listening, flashes back in time and sees his father's hand and the scars.

Remembering all the times he'd missed the lit cigarettes that had burned down between the fingers of his father who'd drunk himself unconscious. He tried to get them all to divert any disaster like starting the house on fire-or awakening the angry bear, lest he forget…

"Burns," he spits as he spins around to Gifford. "Al remembers the claymore, right?"

Then to the rest of the team he yells, "Everybody remembers the claymore, right?"

Everyone, knowing the plan, nods their heads in agreement. It takes Cory another moment to realize there is a problem.

"Oh no." He drops his rucksack and starts walking fast toward the fence, then breaks into a run. Albert's just rounding the storage tank out of sight. Cory picks up speed.

Billy starts to follow and watching Cory, makes a dash to catch up with him.

Cory rounds the corner and seeing Albert, he yells, "Waaaaait!"

Albert freezes and looks back. Cory

stands about thirty feet away.

"Dang it, Al. Don't move. Where are you standing?"

"Dang, Cory," laughs Albert. "Are you trying to give me a heart attack? What are you talking about?"

Nervous and annoyed, Cory barks again, "Just look down! Where are you standing?"

Albert slowly looks down at his feet.

Cory continues. "You got to be close. Do you see it?"

Billy arrives, running around the edge of the storage tank, heading for Cory and Albert.

Cory looks back and seeing him, says, "Get back. Behind that storage tank. Move! You tell the others to stay clear, too."

Billy slowly backs up, turns and signals the others as they approach. Albert is still looking down. Cory knows exactly what Albert is most likely seeing with the trip wire stretched across his ankle.

Laughing quietly, he says, "Cory, I think we may have a problem here. A really big problem. You know what I mean?"

Cory inches closer and fights to stay calm. "Albert, do you see that trip wire or not?"

Sadly amused, Albert says, "Oh yeah. I see it. As a matter of fact, it's right where it's supposed to be. The only problem is, it's stretched across my ankle."

Cory's worst fear is realized. "Dang it, Al," he says on an exhale.

Now in a state of mind to critique himself, Albert says, "You know, we must have rehearsed this mission a hundred times. How could I screw it up?"

Cory starts to move slowly toward Albert. "I don't know. It's okay. It happens, you know?"

Albert suddenly notices Cory getting closer. "Hold it. Just where do you think you're going!?"

Cory freezes in his tracks, then says, "I got to help you, Al."

Angry now, Albert says, "You just stay right there! You got to help me? Tell me, Cory. What's this thing set for? Why don't you just remind me? Refresh my memory?"

Trying to get Albert to settle down, Cory says, "Come on, Al. Give me a break, would ya? Stay calm and we'll figure this out."

Now enraged, Albert fires back, "No! Tell me! I want to hear you say it! Say it!"

Conceding, Cory gives him the information he's begging for. "It's activated by tension and tension release, okay? There, I said it!" Sweat begins to pour off Cory. "Al. You're being a real pain. You know that?"

Albert won't be sidetracked. He knows the truth. "So, basically, I can't move. Is that right? Do I at least have that part right?"

Cory is so concerned and frustrated he yells at his buddy, "Yeah. That's right! So why don't you just shut up a minute and let me come over there and help you?"

He starts walking toward him again but Albert notices and screams.

"Stop McGuire! You just stop moving or I'll trip this thing right here and now! Ya know, I may not be the brightest guy in the world, but I do know a little bit about what's going on here." He pauses a moment to think. "We can't touch this thing, can we?"

Cory, deeply concerned, says quietly, "I don't know, Al. I'm not sure."

After another long pause, Albert lays it out. "So, let me get this straight. You wanna come over here and help me out. Is that right? You want to risk both our lives to do something we both know you can't do?"

"I got to try, Albert," Cory pleads.

"No! You don't gotta do anything! Remember? You don't gotta do nothin'! Why now, man? Why? You never cared before. Why do you care now?"

"I don't know. I don't know! But I'm sure coming over there!"

Cory starts to walk forward again. As tears stream down his face and with fists pointed straight toward Cory, Albert rages, "Aaaaaaaaah! Stopppppp! Just get back!"

Cory can barely think straight. How can he do nothing? How can he watch this and not do something? He screams at Albert, "Dang it, Al! What is your major malfunction?"

In the silence a sudden sense of calm seems to wash over Albert and he says gently, "Look, Cory, I want you to do me a favor. I want you to move over there for a minute. Just a minute. Okay?" He points to a nearby location. Then he continues. "I—I need to think for a second. Just—just give me a second, okay?"

"All right, Al," Cory says, "but you gotta promise me you'll let me in there, you understand?"

"I know. I know. But just give me a second. All right?"

Cory slowly side steps about fifteen feet to the left, closer to the shed. Albert is looking up at the stars for a good minute before he says, "Would you look at that? The sky's cleared up. Not a cloud in sight. You know life's kind of funny that way. You just never know what it's gonna hand you, do ya?"

Still focused upward, he keeps talking softly. "This thing's gonna make a lot of noise when it goes off. It will be no time at all before someone comes to investigate so you boys make sure you get out of here quick. You hear me?"

Cory instinctively starts walking again. "What are you talking about, Al?"

Albert prepares himself. He knows what he needs to do.

"I can't let you do it, Cory. I'm sorry. I'm really sorry I messed this up." Albert faces toward the trip wire and steps forward.

Cory bounds toward him with a primal scream. "Nooooooo!!"

He tackles Albert from behind and they soar through the air as the claymore explodes, lighting up the sky.

Billy's blown backwards from the explosion and crashes against the storage tank. He quickly crawls forward, looks, and seeing the smoke and debris he screams, "McGuirrrrrrrrrrre!"

CHAPTER NINETEEN

IRAQ DESERT - NIGHT

As the Black Hawk helicopter sets down, the team's huddled low to the ground. In the prop wash Gifford barks, "Go! Go! Go! Go!"

The team takes off running toward the helicopter. Several of them carry a casualty. Others swivel from left to right, firing back at a small Iraqi response element that responded to the explosion.

As the chopper blades continue to whip, the gunfire continues. Hand grenades explode, lighting up the sky. The team continues to run, yelling through the deafening roar of the helicopter.

Team members carry a man at a run by his arms and legs to the Black Hawk door. He's bounced up and inside. In an eerie red darkness, they huddle over him.

Parker, on board now, says, "Let's go! Get it up! Get it up!"

Lifting off, the door gunner lays cover fire, spraying bullets back and forth in a sweeping pattern. The team medic rips open gauze packages while others work frantically to save the life of the man on the floor.

The Medic gets down close to his ear. "Hang on! You got to hang on! Don't you quit on me! Do you hear me?"

Hands cover wounds, I.V.'s are being prepped and the men are all yelling at him to make it.

* * *

The wounded Green Beret's hearing starts to fade. A steady, rhythmic beat of his own heart takes over as the Black Hawk flies low and fast over the desert. Lying on the helicopter floor with blood on his face and chest, his breathing is difficult.

He tries to focus. "I—I—just..."

Billy lifts his head into his hands. "Now you just shut up. You're going to make it, you hear me?"

Seemingly delirious, he responds, "His burns. I just — can't stand...burns..."

Confused, Gifford asks Billy, "What's he talking about?"

Billy shrugs. "I don't know, but he does."

Cory strains to sit up. "Albert. Where's Albert?"

Billy shakes his head. "He didn't make it."

Cory surrenders to the medic's urging to lie still. He can feel the tears welling in his eyes.

"Everything I touch doesn't make it," he says.

Billy looks Cory in the face. "That's not true. It wasn't your fault. He forgot the plan. *He* forgot!"

Cory grabs onto Billy's shirt and forces out the words. "He didn't belong here. Why did I do it? Why did I even try?"

"Don't you get it? Don't you see it yet? You've been tryin' to be everybody you're not, man. What you tried to do out there, *that's* what matters."

Cory closes his eyes. He's so tired, but he must make Billy understand. "Al's dead. All he ever wanted me to do was help him out. To give him a break. So, I get him killed. I can't help anyone, even when it counts. Don't you people get that? Don't you?"

Billy looks over at Al's body bag, then back at Cory. He puts his hand on Cory's arm, not even sure Cory can hear him.

"What matters, man, is that you just keep trying. Don't give up on people, buddy. Don't ever."

The medic looks up from his work and finds Gifford. He leaves Cory with Billy, maneuvers his way through the cramped space, and over the loud whine of the helicopter leans in close to Gifford and says, "Zullini took most of the blast." He nods toward Cory. "He's lost a lot of blood, but I'll get him stabilized."

Gifford yells over to Cory, "You're gonna be all right, kid. Good as new."

Then Cory opens his eyes and turns his head to stare at Al's body bag. "Where's my heart lie, Billy? Where's it lie?"

Billy places his finger on Cory's chest. "Right there, buddy. Right there. Smack dab in the middle of your chest. Right? Whether you like it or not, your heart is looking out for people like Al, people like your father, and all the rest of us that need you from time to time, man."

Billy still points at Cory's chest. "That's who you are, Cory, and everybody sees that but you. That's why you went after Al. Don't you see that?"

Cory clenches his fist. "It hurts, brother. I forgot how much it hurts."

"I know it does, buddy." Tearing up, Billy continues. "And I thank God every day that it does because the day we stop feeling is the day it all just don't mean nothing anymore."

Billy reaches out his hand to cover Cory's bandaged one. Cory nods in somber agreement, then closes his eyes.

"Going to miss this team of ours," whispers Billy.

FADE TO BLACK

CHAPTER TWENTY

NINE MONTHS LATER, FORT BRAGG - DAY

Near the statue of the Green Beret who holds out his hand, inside the graduation theater, a man stands in his Class-A uniform.

He stands at the podium wearing his green beret. Three hundred new Green Beret graduates prepare to give a standing ovation as General Richards introduces the speaker.

"Please welcome our guest of honor and Medal of Honor winner, Master Sergeant, retired Jeffrey E. Gettys."

Cory's taxi driver is in his glory, standing proudly with medals and awards covering his chest. The Medal of Honor draped around his neck sits perfectly centered, topping off a uniform of utter perfection.

* * *

At the same time, across the base, over at the demonstration field, another Black Hawk flares hard as it approaches the mock building.

After the maneuvers are completed, it lands on the manicured grass with the mock building smoldering in the background. The engine is turned off and the blades wind down. The doors slide open.

* * *

In the graduation theater, all is quiet as Gettys begins to speak.

"What's it all about? Is it about this here medal around my neck? No, sirs. It is not. It's about you and what I see in a lot of your faces out there. Maybe you are, as I once was, thinking that new patch on your shoulder is like a badge. A badge to symbolize your new-found ruthlessness, your new-found heartlessness, the lone wolf inside of you." He pauses for a long moment. "When your enemy is upon you, that too will have its place..."

* * *

As the chopper blades slowly turn behind them, a small group of men step forward and come to the position of attention.

Parker is first in line, then Gifford, followed by a few more team members. Then Billy steps forward and finally, Cory steps forward, all proudly wearing their green berets.

* * *

In the theater, Gettys continues to address the men with proud and expectant faces.

"But when those bullets be flyin' and those bombs be bustin' all around, killin' your brothers, you learn something alright."

Looking around, he takes a deep breath. "You learn the true meaning of courage. And you learn about the unconditional sacrifice, waiting in all of you, to do what you just do — when or if that moment comes. But recognize before that day comes that there is a hero inside you right now. Not tomorrow, but for today. So be there for your team mates today. Be there for your family today. And be there for your friends, not tomorrow, but today! These are the virtues not easily held on to. And that my friends, is what a hero is. And that my friends, is what true courage and true strength are all about."

* * *

Next to Cory, the last man steps forward. He's a stocky Italian-American and his name tag reads Delluchi. It's demonstration day and the brass, VIP'S, and visitors stand in front of the team with their equipment laid out at their feet.

Cory, with a slight grin, looks over at Delluchi and gives him a nod. Now looking through the crowd Cory recognizes the figure of a man standing alone on the other side of the bleachers.

After a moment, the man signals to Cory with a casual salute of acknowledgment. Cory returns a crisp salute and holds it.

Trotten breaks a smile and slowly lowers his hand.

FADE AWAY FROM THE GREEN BERET STATUE

THE END.

* * *

Back at the LA estate, the Hollywood executive finishes the last page and closes the screenplay. It's still dark outside his window as he sits by the light of his desk lamp. He hasn't taken more than a short coffee break since he opened the first pages.

He places it back into the brown envelope and shoves it off to the corner of his desk. Behind him on the wall are several posters for the blockbuster movies he's been part of. The entire office is decorated like an Academy Awards showroom of achievements. Photographs and autographs of celebrities, trophies and plaques are on display.

With a few contemplative taps of his pen on the edge of his desk, he reaches over and turns the lamp off.

He needs some rest but is looking forward to making a few phone calls in the morning.

"Where the Heart Lies" is in his heart but he also knows there is more to the story.

CHAPTER TWENTY-ONE

A few days later, a man in his late forties answers his phone.

"Yes, this is Cory McGuire. Who's calling?"

The Hollywood executive introduces himself. "Mr. McGuire, I'd like you to come see me about your screenplay. I have been thinking about your story quite a bit and I must admit, I am intrigued. Are you interested?" he asks.

Cory thinks a moment. It's been many years since he's spoken of the story he wrote years before. It's been in his bottom desk drawer for a long time. His military life is behind him and he's tried to move on. But like some other strange events in his life, this could be important. Maybe he can make better sense of his career and finally put to rest the life he once lived.

"Yes sir, I'm interested. When would you like to meet?"

After discussing the dates and arrangements, Cory hangs up the phone and goes into his study.

He takes a seat and looks around the room as though it's a new place. He notices the pictures and military memorabilia on his walls. He stares at the folded flag he received upon discharge and smiles at his chipped and scratched helmet sitting on the shelf.

As he thinks about the upcoming Hollywood meeting, memories about all that inspired him to write the story in the first place flood his mind. It has been a while since he's thought about the story, his career, and the Army.

He leans back and closes his eyes to remember.

* * *

Week fifteen of Special Forces School and he had no idea how he'd survived any of it. It never seemed to get easier. Silence trapped the night. All that he could hear was the rain splashing down onto his green poncho shelter. The rhythmic sounds of steady dripping somehow provided a strange sense of peace and calm.

It was night and the once-swollen clouds finally retreated and a slight pushing breeze took over. It signaled that the North Carolina storm had ceased and would send no more long, crackling streaks of lighting or peels of angry thunder to shake the pine trees and forest around him.

He peeked out from beneath the only comfort he had, his well-worn Army poncho. Clouds raced to the north and beyond, and bright stars shone between the thick clouds.

The moon broke through and illuminated the dense forest floor. As the large drops of water fell, puddles of trapped rain made puddles that weighed down his shelter.

In the distance, but not too far off, he heard another sound. It was the bulky, long whip antenna PRC 77 radio squelching, "Chuuuuuuuu.... Chuuuuuuuu."

Peering off in its direction, he saw a faint glow from the fluorescent green chem light that hung from the antenna's tip. Chilled and soaking wet on the saturated forest floor, he noted the comfort of the thick pine needle-covered ground. He saw other mound-like shelters with steam rising from them which marked the warmth escaping the soldiers hunkered beneath. This was a good reminder that he wasn't alone and trainees like him were lying under their own ponchos. He put his head back inside his cocoon and soon drifted off to sleep.

It was 12:30 a.m. when he got a tug on his poncho. He pulled the flap from over his head and the rain puddles washed his face, but he was so wet, what did it matter? At least the great deluge had stopped.

An occasional squelch still crackled from the radio and it reminded him of what he was about to do. At 1:00 a.m. exactly six of them would be handed their first set of coordinates. A ten hour, 28-kilometer land navigation test was set to begin. It was an individual event: they'd have to rely solely on their own wits and abilities to get through this one.

He'd done well with the far shorter distances but this one had him nervous. They had to find all four points in the short time allotted. If he failed, he had to leave the school. All that hard work could be for nothing. He'd either be "recycled," made to start the entire Special Forces cycle over again by joining in with the next class or be dropped entirely from Special Forces training. The thought of repeating the entire fifteen weeks was too terrible to imagine.

The test was called the "STAR" exam and it was the most intimidating for all the students. Fifty to sixty percent usually failed. The terrain was unpredictable and varied from clear pine forests to thick vegetated swampland like the infamous Bones Fork Creek. The moonlight provided little assistance for the night movement ahead. It turned everything into ghostly images offering only an eerier sense of loneliness to come.

As he tucked his equipment away he could hear the other

candidates doing the same. They weren't allowed to talk to each other. The green chem light hanging above the instructor's head provided a strange sense of comfort. It was the only thing shining in that dark Carolina forest.

At 1:00 a.m. the instructor started calling them over. Cory had laid out his equipment before dark, so he could find it, that way it would not take him long to be ready.

The instructor called out for McGuire.

He put on his seventy-pound rucksack and moved out to his location. The sergeant then gave him an eight-digit grid coordinate. He read it back to him and the instructor wished him good luck.

Moving away, Cory bent over and began to plot his course. His heart felt like it was beating out of his chest. This was it. Pass it or fail, the time was now. He checked and rechecked. The slightest miscalculation meant being several hundred meters off target. His first leg was over a ten-kilometer movement.

They were told that when they reached their "needle in a haystack" point they'd find an instructor sitting next to a tree. The tree would have a four inch, red-painted ring, six-feet up the trunk. Since it would still be dark as pitch, he didn't think that knowledge would help him much.

He shot his first magnetic azimuth of 148 degrees on his compass. The filament, which provided his only light, contrasted the darkness around him. As he went one direction, others passed him going in another.

Cory took off running, smashing through branches and jumping over bushes and logs. Though ten hours sounded like a long time, all four points could never be found by strolling along and he'd learned that a long time ago.

Precise, pinpoint accuracy had to be accomplished at a high

rate of speed. Any mistake would cost valuable minutes that at least fifty percent of them didn't have to waste.

He had to pick terrain features along the way as checkpoints - a ridge line, a road crossing, or the number of power lines overhead to confirm his route. The compass only served as a directional guide to get you to those places. When he got close – about 500 meters – he'd have to find his last unmistakable terrain feature corresponding to the map called an "attack point." From there, he'd be nose to the compass walking exactly the right number of steps in an exact direction–or miss his target and fail.

If he needed to take his time to be precise, that would be the place to do it.

* * *

Around 0500 a.m. Cory arrived at his attack point. He had traveled four hours through the dark and rain-soaked underbrush to get there, seeing no one along the way. The lights of a distant town or small city helped confirm his general direction because he'd seen it on the map.

From the attack point, Cory walked in the direction the instructor point was supposed to be. The terrain became more dense, dark, and descended at a sharp decline.

The air became cooler and the sounds of brush more muffled. Not even able to see his hand in front of his face he carefully moved forward like a blind man. He checked and rechecked his compass. His distance traveled, or pace count, had to be precise. Whatever was in front of him, he had to walk over, push through, or crawl under. He could not deviate from the precise compass reading. As Cory finished counting the paces to the instructor point, he stopped. There was nothing there. He just stood in a thick brush depression in disbelief. Was he completely off course? Had he made a tragic error in his map plotting or utilization of check points? He didn't know.

All his senses were heightened. What he heard, smelled, and felt were all being analyzed instantly. At the same time, a sixth sense of sorts guided him. Cory fought off the panic. If he was an instructor, would he go into even deeper underbrush to set up a point? Not likely.

Conducting a 360-degree turn, Cory looked in every direction. After reviewing it in his mind, he was confident he was in the right place. Indecisiveness, doubt, or panic had no place in Special Forces and certainly not while standing miles from civilization in a deep, dark place. His sixth sense allowed him to consider one last idea.

Maybe the instructor point was obscured by trees or vines. Cory got down on one knee where he could see from a different vantage point. He looked to his right, and where he'd looked while standing up a moment ago, he suddenly saw the glow of a green chem light. He walked toward it, never taking his eyes off the green orb. It was so obscure he was afraid he'd lose sight of it should a branch or tree get between him and the light. Within twenty meters he was standing at the foot of the instructor's tree.

A whole one-man camp was there, and a radio squelched. About six feet up the tree, the light hung.

Cory felt like he'd found all of civilization. The instructor just looked at him with indifference. "I could hear you out there and was wondering if you'd make it."

Cory handed him his slip of paper and sounded off with his student number.

He only had six more hours to find three more points. With a new set of coordinates, Cory realized he had about the same distance to cover with his new coordinates. He pointed his compass and moved into the dark and away from the comfort of the green orb and the indifferent instructor.

Running and jumping, clicking beads down on his pace count cord, checking and rechecking his compass readings, Cory attacked the thick forest striving to make up time. The sunrise gave him an added advantage for speed and checkpoint verifications.

Sweat mingled with the rain that he'd collected from every branch, bush and limb. Cory felt the weight of his rucksack on his shoulders and the fatigue starting to set in. He'd had less than three hours sleep in the last thirty-six hours.

As the sun rose, the heat and humidity of the day quickly materialized. On his next point he was slightly off again and made a search until he found it. He had three hours left.

The atmosphere buzzed with the extreme heat. It was July in North Carolina and to say it was "hot" running with full gear over hills and through fields was an understatement. Cory's body had been going at one hundred percent for hours. Wearing thick fatigues, overheating was inevitable.

Again, he ran, running out of water in his canteens. He knew disaster could befall him, so he made a conscious decision to go all out. He knew the risk he was taking for getting a heat stroke, but he didn't care. He'd gone too far to stop short of the goal.

Cory's third point came quickly, but he had only forty-five minutes to find his last point. He had several kilometers to cover and couldn't make any mistakes.

With so little time, he didn't take the time to fill his canteen. Across open fields, up and over hills, and through pockets of forests, Cory moved as fast and as accurately as he could. He saw what he hoped was the last two-kilometer field. Everything in him screamed to stop before he boiled over.

He'd stopped sweating from severe dehydration, but again he

made a conscious decision to put it all on the line. He ran harder and faster as if sprinting to a finish line.

Fifteen-hundred meters later, his face deep red and his lungs burning, Cory stopped at the trees on the other side of the long field. It was at the end of his pace count.

He didn't immediately see any sign of an instructor's location and Cory had no idea how much time he had left, but he most likely didn't have time to be off target. Right then he heard "report over here."

Bent over to catch his breath, Cory looked to his immediate right and saw his point location less than ten meters away. There were several other students already there sitting and resting against their packs. He moved to the instructor and handed him his piece of paper.

"You cut it close. You have about ten minutes left."

Cory collapsed in the shade and his legs instantly cramped up. The other students just looked at him as he guzzled down a fresh canteen of water. He had survived.

Not long after Cory had reported in, an Army truck came to pick them up. Getting back to the assembly area Cory saw hundreds of students sitting or milling about. He got off the truck and started moving toward the big crowd.

An instructor hollered, "Not that group. That's the test failures. Yours is the smaller one over there."

The smaller crowd had about forty students. They'd lost seventy-five percent of the class. Cory was one of the few to pass the land navigation test. As he took a more detailed look at the groups, he noticed the failed group included students wearing splints, head dressings, eye patches and I.V.s.

Every aspect of Special Forces training was extreme. Extreme land navigation, extreme rucksack marches, and extreme explosives training. The school didn't do anything half way. Like SFAS, instructors were still evaluating.

Some students passed, some failed, and some were sent back to start with a new class. There were several sergeants' specialties in Special Forces. They were designed, so no matter where a team might be dropped off in the world, they could be self-sufficient for conducting training and to conduct operations.

The core specialties were the Weapons Sergeant, Engineer Sergeant, Communications Sergeant, and Medical Sergeant. Cory was in the Engineer program. In addition to learning all phases of constructing roads, bridges, and structures, he was also taught to be an expert in demolitions and explosives.

For several weeks he spent time in a classroom or on an explosives range. In the classroom, after learning bridge design, he learned bridge destruction. The proper type, amount, and placement of the explosives charge had to be calculated. Doing that required an in-depth understanding of how bridges and other structures were built. The level of delaying or denying the enemy determined the level of destruction required.

Every day Cory was tasked with working out exact mathematical equations and formulas that supported a given mission. The Engineer Sergeants had to be familiar with all types of anti-personnel and vehicle mines. The pace was fast and mistakes equaled dismissal. Failure to meet course standards meant leaving the course.

Out of the original thirty-plus students, only Cory and seven others moved on.

CHAPTER TWENTY-TWO

Cory remembered the third phase of Special Forces school. None of the phases got any easier and at every turn, he was sure he'd fail out. Maybe that's what saw him through it all. He didn't know how to quit, but he didn't know how he'd ever start over at it, either. Master Sergeant Trotten was never too far away from Cory in thought or conversation. After all, it was he who inspired him to not quit on himself. The pain of losing his father was replaced with a resolve to find another reason to live. Trotten was key to that. To Cory he was like the father he never had.

* * *

Standing in the dark on the lowered tailgate of a C-130, Cory remembers the hills and trees race out of sight below him. There was an extra 230 pounds of rucksack dangling at his knees and parachute equipment hanging off his back. Camouflage paint crisscrossed his face and he held onto his parachute static line cord to steady himself.

The plane dipped violently in the thick air turbulence and banked back and forth carving a path low over the North Carolina countryside.

Men stood one behind the other and a single red light dimly lit the interior of the aircraft. The sound of the wind and engines were too loud to yell over. Cory's eyes burned from the plane's exhaust fumes. His back screamed from trying to keep the 180-pound rucksack up. The pain was so severe he just wanted to jump out the aft end of the plane already. He couldn't wait to be ripped into the jet stream to be relieved of the pain.

Phase three. Cory and his mock twelve-man operational detachment (alpha), or ODA, were conducting a training mission. The task was to jump in undetected behind enemy lines and set up a "hide site" or hidden reconnaissance to watch a major enemy supply route.

For a week, the ODA team had researched, planned, and rehearsed the mission. Every aspect of the training mission was to be treated as real. As the engineer, Cory had to come up with a hide site construction plan. Exact amounts of materials had to be parachuted in with the team. In addition, each man carried at least nine quarts, or two gallons of water. Everything had to be jumped in: food, water, ammunition, hide site materials, and all manner of tactical equipment.

Suddenly the lights turned from red to green. The first man jumped into a sea of black and the faint silhouette of his opening parachute could be seen. The pack tray of the parachute and its cord whipped in the jet stream, slamming against the sides of the ramp opening. One by one, jumping one step behind the man in front of them, they lunged off the ramp.

Cory followed the line taking him to the black hole and forcefully stepped out. For a moment, he was violently washed around in the air current. He lost his stomach from the instant drop. He counted to himself, almost willing his chute to rip open.

A few seconds later, he felt the gliding, lifting effect of a full canopy over his head. Total silence rushed into his senses as he watched the ghostly outline of the aircraft fade out of his vision. All around him, above and below, he could see the other chutes floating down across the sky. Cory steered into the wind and gradually saw the countryside increase in detail. He saw the drop zone below in an open field. The darkness revealed only a slightly different color from the thick bush that surrounded it.

Closer and closer, faster and faster, the ground rushed up toward him. Reaching down, he pulled his single point release strap and watched his rucksack fall to the end of its line. It dangled twenty feet below swaying from side to side.

Pulling his steering toggle, Cory made one last turn to make sure he was faced into the wind. The ground became instantly more intimate. At first, it was just a view from above, but quickly it turned into a personal reality.

Treetops, limbs, and bushes were all revealed in simultaneous detail. The knee-high grass suddenly took shape and the speed of impact rapidly advanced.

Cory braced for the landing, putting his feet together and tucking his elbows in. His whole body tried to anticipate the controlled crash.

He heard his rucksack make impact, and then gritted his teeth. Hitting the ground forced the air out of his lungs and he grunted with the pain of impact.

His feet stung, then his hip absorbed the full weight of his body landing. The forward momentum made him fall onto his shoulder and back like an out of control tumbler. The crashing ended, and he laid still. The parachute fluttered down and quietly descended to the grass next to him.

Sounds of the countryside filled his ears and he could smell the fragrance of the moist field. The airborne operation was over.

His body soaked in sweat, Cory's uniform stuck to his skin. He had recovered his rucksack and pulled it over his shoulders. It seemed heavier than it had before. Every one of the twelve-man team assembled nearby in a wooded area, quiet as ghosts. No one spoke; only a gesture or quick arm signal was necessary. Everyone understood their assignment. Still too dark to see, they silently filed through the underbrush and disappeared into the forest.

They walked all night and stopped only to conduct silent map checks and to cross danger areas so they remained undetected. At times, they only moved a few hundred meters. Slow, silent, and methodical, they kept going forward. With each passing hour, their packs dug deeper into their muscles until the straps felt like they were resting on shoulder and collar bones. Cory's knees ached from kneeling whenever they halted.

On a slight, almost invisible trail, a whisper was passed back down the line. It was one word: "hole," spoken face to face.

Each member trusted what they heard and walked around the questionable depression in the earth. Cory passed the word back to the man behind him.

The team member heard the word "hold."

The file continued. However, the team member that held back lost sight of his group and decided to move quickly to catch up. He was instantly swallowed up by the massive hole.

The full hundred-eighty pounds carefully balanced between his shoulder blades shifted and accelerated him into the void. Stumbling, he managed to catch himself after several half-steps. The pain traveled down his shoulders and spine to his hips and knees. Recovering, he fell back in step. There was no crying, whimpering, or anger. No emotional outburst. It was something to be ignored–a non-issue. The mission was all that mattered.

As the sun began to rise, the team descended into their patrol base. It was a thick layer of vines, brush, and low-hanging tree branches. They would blend into their surroundings. Once again, a quick hand signal was made, and each man spread out to form a circular perimeter.

Kneeling or laying behind a fallen log or other concealing piece of vegetation, everyone scanned his sector. Weapons faced out, ready to suppress any assault or ambush.

Whichever the direction of an attack, the team was ready to respond and reinforce that side of the line of defense. It was so quiet, Cory could hear if a twig snapped a hundred feet away.

Finally, another hand and arm signal went around the perimeter and the team began the next stage. In the center of the circle an operations center was set up. Security elements were pushed out to serve as a listening and observation team. Convinced of their relative safety and security, the team decreased their security posture to prepare for the next phase of the operation.

According to the map, they were just a few kilometers from their chosen hide site location. They moved around as little as possible, only doing the necessary radio checks or taking drinks of water to stay hydrated. Equipment for the night movement was quietly pre-positioned for ease of identification after dark. The daylight hours passed slowly in the heavy, hot North Carolina air. The sun marched from one end of the sky to the other. Twelve hours passed and aside from a few recon missions, the team stayed in place. They waited until the day became night when they could once again own the darkness.

* * *

It was time. Cory had cross loaded everything the team would need to set up and occupy the hide-site. Each man carried what was specific to his role for quickly getting the job done.

The team had to trust Cory. He'd researched and practiced the exact formula for constructing the hide-site. Regardless, they didn't understand the unconventional means by which Cory prepared them.

Besides carrying enough food, water, and recon equipment to last several days inside a concealed hole, some of the men carried metal electrical conduit poles, chicken wire, tarps and sandbags. Most confusing was the requirement to carry full black trash bags of pine needles which were collected just outside the patrol base.

When it was safe enough to move, a team of six, including Cory, moved carefully to the site's location. Advance teams were sent ahead to observe for any signs of enemy forces. The training scenario required infiltration deep behind enemy lines; being detected or having their security compromised were not options.

They spotted the major supply road they needed to monitor. One hundred and fifty meters behind the road were mounds that naturally covered the pine-forested hillside.

Above the road and amongst the mounds, they'd build their hide-site. One of the prerequisites for the mission was to leave behind no sign of having been there.

The six-man team filed down the hill the last hundred feet to the location Cory had chosen from aerial photos he'd studied. Luckily, the plan was simple because in the limited time and visibility they had to work with, there was no room for complicated schemes. The team took off their rucksacks and laid out their equipment. At the same time, Cory and few others started quietly digging. They dug a cave so they could hide beneath the ground. Cory measured and staked out the nine by nine-foot square which had to be dug. He solved the problem of leaving any traces or taking too long to make the hide site by having every shovel full of dirt that came out be placed into a sand bag. The full sandbags would then be placed around the edges of the square hole.

Digging three feet deep, they were able to pile three feet high worth of sandbags for a total of six feet then available for use. Once that was complete, the thinner diameter metal poles were slid out from the thicker ones and extended to cover one end of the square. Cory bent the poles in the middle and then taped them where they all crossed at the apex forming a tent frame. Then the team rolled out sections of chicken wire and laid them over the frame.

After that, they spread thick plastic tarps over the frame to complete the tent-like construction. Cory formed the poles and chicken wire in such a way to appear rounded and like the other mounds. Finally, the men emptied the pine straw from their garbage bags over the entire structure, spreading and blending it in with the rest of the natural ground cover.

Within thirty minutes, the hide-site was complete and there was one more mound added to the hillside. Inside, two to three men remained hidden in relative comfort for days. Two coffee cans were shoved through the front of the hide site and camouflaged to enable them to see through. Inside, they recorded all activity occurring on the road.

They ate, drank, and slept in the site.

As the first team inserted, Cory and the rest of the team sealed them in by closing the back of the hide-site. Then they crawled back the way they came in. As they retreated, they brushed all the disturbed ground back into place, covering any signs.

Back at the edge of the thicket they took one last look. In the foreground they saw the silhouette of a hill dotted with pine straw mounds. They had secretly designed, constructed, and inserted an invisible team to conduct surveillance.

As it turned out, that was the easy part. living in the hole and lying still for two to three days recording any and all activity was the hard part.

CHAPTER TWENTY-THREE

After he finished Special Forces school, Cory was assigned to Fort Campbell and 5th Special Forces Group (SFG) located in Clarksville, Tennessee, about forty-five minutes northwest of Nashville.

Fort Campbell was also home to the 101st Infantry. Both units were legendary. The 101st was instrumental in WWII and were chronicled in the "Band of Brothers" series. The 5th SFG was highly successful in Vietnam, as was the 101st. 5th Group earned numerous unit citations and nineteen Congressional Medals of Honor.

In the late 1960s, John Wayne led the financing, production, and starred in a movie about an Army unit called, "The Green Berets," which became a classic. Several years after that war ended, 5th Group moved, making its home a few streets down from the 101st.

Built sometime in the 1960s, the buildings they occupied were tan, three-story, cinderblock construction. Offices, arms rooms and storage areas occupied the first floor and basement levels. The second and third floors were designated for the twelve-man team rooms and offices. In between the buildings, pull up bars, logs, and climbing ropes were set into place. A large parade field of grass sat in the middle like a football field. By the time Cory arrived there in late 1995, the place looked old and neglected.

He reported to his new permanent unit there and his new Sergeant Major. The company sergeant major's office was at the end of the hall directly across from the commander's office. Inside were an Army-standard heavy gray desk, a few filing cabinets, a couple of tired chairs, and a vinyl covered couch, also Army issued.

The faded Army-issued linoleum tile floor in the old 1960s-era building was dull and scuffed all the way into the sergeant major's office. Cory stood in the center of the office and the sergeant major was behind his desk. They studied the dry erase board on the wall. Various colors were used to note dates, names, numbers, and box-lettered matrixes.

With his hands behind his head, the sergeant major leaned back and asked, "So. What kind of team do you want to go on?"

Looking at the board Cory paused. He glanced at Sergeant Major. "What about the HALO team?"

"No. Doesn't look like we have any open positions with the Sky Dive crew." He laughed. "Everyone wants on that team."

"Yes, Sergeant Major, I know. But I figured it was worth a try," Cory said.

Again, they stared at the board in silence. "What about the SCUBA team?" he asked Cory.

Pondering it for a moment, he wondered what that was all about. Would that be a poor choice? If it meant hanging out on beaches, it couldn't be that bad, could it?

At the same time, the sergeant major began trying to sell him on it. That should have been a big red flag, but Cory was too naive to recognize the danger.

He found himself saying, "All right, Sergeant Major, that sounds pretty good."

The Sergeant Major broke into a grin and got to his feet. Without hesitation, he congratulated Cory on a fine decision.

"Okay then. Go down the hall and report to 575. Tell them I sent you."

* * *

Cory knocked on the team room door that was decorated with an assortment of Great White shark images and other dive-related objects. All of a sudden, the whole dive team thing felt a little foreboding to him.

Up until then, most of the guys he'd met in the SF were mellow and polite. His world was about to change. The door flew open and Cory was immediately confronted with an aggressive, fraternity-type atmosphere. Several team members in various stages of uniform or exercise clothes were sitting or standing around a large table in the middle of the team room.

"Sergeant Major said to come down here and report to you guys."

As if in disbelief, one of the team members smiled and shook his head. "You want to be on a SCUBA team? And the sergeant major sent you down here?"

They all burst out laughing as though that was the funniest thing they'd ever heard, but there was also a new excitement in the air. A "fresh meat" kind of excitement. Cory had no idea what he was getting himself in to. He thought it was scuba diving and might be relaxing, entertaining with coral reefs abounding. He had no idea he had volunteered for the US Army Special Forces brand of the Navy Seals.

When the laughter died down, there were questions like, "Can you swim?" "Ever dive before?" "Can you hold your breath a long time?"

Every answer he gave just made the guys laugh and shake their heads. It was the kind of laughter and attention he didn't want to get. Cory was hoping to leave a better first impression. Whatever kind of experience he said he had only made things worse.

After the introductions and jokes started to subside, Cory seemingly became invisible in the room. The team started talking about him like he wasn't even there. They were forming a plan and strategizing how to save his life or at least forestall Cory's death for a time.

"So, I guess we can take him out and see how his run times are?"

"We'll have to schedule the pool. Make sure someone calls them. Oh yeah. Make sure you bring the medic kit."

"How fast do you think we can get him ready?"

"I don't know. He looks—well, it depends on how strong of a swimmer he is."

"Somebody start looking for Pre-SCUBA schools."

After a length of time, when they finished working everything out, they looked around looking for Cory who was still standing right where they'd left him.

After a pause, one of them smiled and said, "Ready!?"

In Cory's naivety, he'd signed up for what very few others in SF are capable of accomplishing: earning the coveted "SCUBA Bubble" badge. Over the next three months he would be sorely tested.

When the team brought him to the pool for the first time, he thought they were joking. The indoor swimming pool on post was an eerie place. It was old, dark, humid, the water deep, and the pool long. Once he was in the water, he demonstrated his basic swimming skills.

After that, Cory was asked to swim underwater from one end of the 25-meter pool and back again. That is half the length of a football field. He thought they were just harassing him. There was no way that could be a real requirement; accomplishing that would be impossible.

They also wanted him to put on twin 80 dive tanks, a buoyancy compensator floatation collar, a weight belt with 18 pounds, and a mask and fins. Cory's job was to move away from the wall of the pool into the deep end, put his hands in the air, and keep his head above water somehow for five minutes. He got a little angry that the team was fooling with him so much. There was no way that could be a requirement. And there was absolutely no way that task was humanly possible anyway.

They just smiled and laughed at him. As best they could, they relayed to him that the requirements were real and that they were not kidding. They also wanted Cory to tie ropes together on the bottom of the pool, ultimately tying three separate knots together connecting two very short ropes where the last knot was almost impossible to complete. It seemed the task could take a few minutes while you kneeled on the bottom of the pool struggling with the stiff ropes.

Another exercise was to take all your dive gear off a few pieces at a time and lay them very neatly on the bottom of the pool in a perfect predetermined arrangement. Then he had to try to dive down and put all the gear on with a single breath completing the task by donning his dive mask, clearing *all* the water out of it, and finally slowly fin to the surface blowing little bubbles all the way up. Another impossible feat.

To say he was humbled that first day in the pool would be an understatement. The team was satisfied that they'd finally conveyed to Cory the enormity of what he'd signed up for. He was left lying on the pool deck, soaking wet, in shock, humiliated, and feeling like his head was going to explode.

It was January in Tennessee, and the team prepared Cory the best they could for a few more weeks. He ran until he puked, did pushups, sit-ups, and rope climbs until he could do no more. He spent several hours a day in the pool. The idea of swimming the length of half a football field on a single breath seemed more possible every day. By the end, he was dragging a weight belt while he scratched at the bottom of the pool to get to the other end and back, ever increasing his breath-holding capacity.

Within a few weeks of continuous training Cory was faster, stronger, and more capable of accomplishing the impossible water tasks. He even managed to feel somewhat at peace in the water while it became his new home.

Drown Proofing: Hands tied behind the back and feet bound together was a twenty-minute water-survival exercise. Even that task he found more comfortable in the final days. As the team looked for pre-SCUBA classes being held somewhere, Cory was secretly praying they wouldn't find one. He needed a whole lot more time. He was not ready. Cory didn't imagine one could ever feel ready for that experience.

* * *

A short, stocky, pit bull of a team sergeant and his equally sadistic team were in charge of the class. SF guys came from all over the country. The course was run under strict guidelines and was meant to better prepare potential SF Combat Divers for SCUBA school.

Those who didn't pass or weren't recommended to attend SCUBA school had sacrificed so much and worked hard but would go home empty handed. They would not advance.

CHAPTER TWENTY-FOUR

It was cold. O'dark-thirty at Fort Bragg in February was not arctic-cold, but pretty cold nonetheless. Cory met the rest of the pre-SCUBA class on a football field bordered by a quarter-mile running track.

A few of the overhead lamps dimly illuminated the area. Everyone wore black wool caps and kept moving to stay warm in their gray Army sweats. That's where they met their class cadre, all friendly but professional.

In total, there were ten to twelve instructors and approximately thirty students. Cory watched their breath steam out as everyone started stretching. They had to perform yet another PT test. It seemed like every time he saw Fort Bragg a PT test was required. All the normal maximum effort, including nausea, muscle failure and burning lungs accompanied the PT test experience.

Not being totally familiar with Fort Bragg and trying to find his way around brought added stress and intensity to his training. After the PT test, Cory was given an address to report to, a drop-dead time to be there, and information regarding what uniform to wear and what equipment to bring. With a map in one hand and a steering wheel in the other, he raced through the streets and barracks areas hoping he'd land at the desired destination at the right time.

From the PT test, Cory raced back to the old military hotel called Moon and Hardy Hall, ran upstairs, changed, grabbed gear, ate on the way, then drove back across post and reported to an indoor, glass-enclosed swimming pool.

Every day was the same routine. Jump out of the car, pre-stage their equipment on the pool deck, offload scuba tanks and other gear out of the instructor's vehicles being careful not to fall on the ice and snow, then make it to formation standing behind the gear, wearing mask, weight belt, and fins hanging from the straps over his wrists.

Cory always seemed to have about a half-second left before he was officially over the allotted time to be ready. He spent approximately eleven hours a day training. It was really a *selection* course. Whoever could not adapt, keep up, or was injured had to leave.

With increasing levels of difficulty added at planned intervals throughout the course, some candidates were ready to advance and others not so much. Daily, Cory watched the drama unfold: coughing or puking and holding onto the side of the pool while instructors yelled at students to "release the side of the pool." Others nearly drowned in the middle when they couldn't tread and keep their heads up. Some passed out when they got half-way across the bottom of the pool to get to the other side on a single breath.

All punishment came in a frenzy of yelling and screaming while candidates did flutter kicks on the side of the pool so their fins slapped the water. The instructors filled their masks with hose water and soaked them down like they were adrift on a ship. Sometimes sit-ups and push-ups while wearing scuba tanks were required. It was all designed to cause one thing: muscle failure.

When Cory could not hold his breath any longer, he had to find a way. Or when he couldn't keep himself afloat or swim another stroke, he had to find a way. The only break he could take was on the bottom of the pool because that seemed like the place the instructors wanted them anyway.

Every day the pool had fewer candidates in it. Guys either happily quit or left with injuries. It was a gradual thing. But one day, it seemed like half the class grabbed the side of the pool and crawled out quitting just relieved to have escaped death. It was a bad day with drama and chaos in the pool. The building echoed with drowning sounds, screaming, choking, people scratching at the surface to find air and flailing to survive.

The students needed each other to make it through, but after a while, Cory realized he couldn't depend on anyone because they might be gone at any minute.

It seemed that everyone could handle the events for the most part, but it was when they were required to perform them faster, longer, and with added stress that made the difference. But that was the point of the training: to surrender to the fear of running out of air.

To be a good combat diver, one must reach the point where the body stops fighting to survive. The pain fades away once they stop straining, panicking, gulping, or contracting the lungs. A ringing sound becomes louder and louder while sight gets narrower and narrower. All the while, a SCUBA member calmly continues to work out the problem of untying or completing the task until he blacks out.

After the pool work, they were given the standard zero time

to get to their next location. They raced back to their rooms, changed, got something to eat, then grabbed a map and went on the hunt for the elusive next location. Usually they had to stop at an area to climb thick ropes strung high between telephone poles. Three or four times they had to get up and back down.

From there, they flew down the roads through the "back forty" ranges on a long thirty or forty-minute drive to Mott Lake. There they would jump out of the car with bags of equipment and suit up in full wet suits, hoodies, booties, gloves, weight belts, floatation collars, masks, buddy lines, and buoys.

To warm them up for the thirty-eight-degree water, copious amounts of exercise would commence. Like grass drills, they jumped, rolled, did push-ups, flutter kicks, rolling, mountain climbers and jumping jacks, also known as the side-straddle hop. The warm up "death sessions" would be conducted until complete muscle failure was achieved and all were drenched in sweat and broiling heat.

Cory couldn't wait to get in that freezing water. So far, they'd been lucky. He'd heard about other classes that had to break ice to perform the swims. The task was to swim on their side with one arm stretched out while finning as fast as they could from one end of the lake, around the corner, down to the other end, and back. There was a time standard and they performed as a buddy team.

They swam for two to four hours and by the time they finished, Cory couldn't stand up. Before the day was through there were more punishing exercises to do, clean up to complete, equipment to load, and the drive back to the boat house/dive locker.

Once at the dive locker building, every piece of equipment had to be cleaned, deflated, stacked, washed, and scrubbed, as they watched the sun go down. With a few more rounds of exercise they were finally sent back to their rooms to eat and get a few hours of sleep.

By the time the final day arrived, Cory had spent hundreds of hours in the pool, run sub-six-minute miles all over Fort Bragg, conducted thousands of push-ups, flutter kicks, pull-ups, and climbed several hundred feet of rope.

He needed a medic to give him a shot to numb his right hip flexor to dampen the sharp pain caused by the over exertion from finning so much. He wasn't sure exactly when it happened, but Cory suddenly realized most of the other students were gone. After a blur of two plus weeks Cory stood in formation on graduation day with the last three survivors.

Standing next to him were the "D boys," men from CAG or more commonly known as Delta Force, though they never told him that. He found out by asking someone else because they couldn't officially talk about it.

They looked fit and strong. The only time Cory remembered seeing them look a little worried was on the last pool event when they had to repeat the "tank tread" with twin 80s on their backs, weight belts, and hands up out of the water.

Although he was still standing, another SF guy was experiencing an allergic reaction to the chlorine where his eyes were severely blood shot and watering. He wasn't given a passing grade but got a certificate instead that basically meant "thanks for showing up."

Cory and the two Delta Force operators received the coveted "recommendation to attend the Combat Diver course." Their tremendous success was marked only by their standing tall in a rare three-man formation under a cold, gray February morning on a lonely parade field in Fort Bragg. After an unceremonious graduation, they said their goodbyes with a few quiet handshakes.

He had little time to congratulate himself as he was already thinking and worrying about the real SCUBA school down in Florida. He was just hoping he would make it. He had a lonely and quiet ten-hour drive to convince himself that there was no other option.

CHAPTER TWENTY-FIVE

A few months later, Cory was in Key West, Florida, at Trumbo Point Annex and half-way through Dive School. He ate over ten-thousand calories a day but was as skinny as the rest who burned every calorie in the twenty-four-hour training cycle.

In the darkness the dive boat bobbed in the ocean. The engines idled and smoke formed a thin layer of smog on the surface. Two by two, like ghostly silhouettes, the dive buddy teams sat on the side of the boat ready to flip over the side. They wore the Draeger rebreather system with two black hoses running from the mouth piece. They were holding lines and buoys. The masks on their faces were slightly fogged up as they breathed through the astronaut-like apparatuses.

"Enter the water!" the instructor commanded.

They flipped over the side in pairs and the boat backed down as the divers disappeared near the bow of the boat. They got one last compass reading, gave a thumbs-down signal, and disappeared.

The beach could barely be seen. A pre-stationed vehicle with the headlights on were all they had to guide them. At eighteen feet below, just above the sand and grass bottom, there was no light except the illumination from the green glow-stick attached to their compass board. On the board was also a watch and depth gauge. They swam strictly dependent upon what those devices were reading. It was not unlike flying an aircraft solely by instrumentation.

Side by side they knew they were together only by touch. Inches off the bottom, they finned fast and silent in the direction the compass heading indicated. They finned and finned while continually checking their gauges and oxygen levels. Their breathing was fast and heavy, like running a pace for five miles. The rebreather kept cycling the same breath over and over, filtering it through the granules to make it breathable again.

A high pitch sound could be heard on occasion informing them that now the Draeger was mixing a bit of new oxygen with the stale recycled breath. It was always like breathing half a breath. The lungs wanted so much more, but the small rebreather bag only provided so much volume. Nevertheless, they continued to fin.

The beach never seemed to come. Their legs screamed with burning pain as they dove, pushing the water and propelling their fins through the water. The sweat and heat were almost unbearable. Waves of anxiety assaulted Cory.

Is the compass broken? Have we stayed on heading? Is there enough breathable air left in the system? Am I going to pass out? Is the rig failing and poisoning me? Can I keep going at this pace? Are we close?

Hours went by in darkness and silence except for the sound of Cory's own rhythmic breathing. His ears started to perceive a change in pressure, and the water temperature changed slightly. The debris passing his hands and face changed too. Slowly the depth gauge rose in feet.

Another hour passed. Cory slowed down so they did not disturb the surface. They advanced forward and finally were at knee high level. They ascended together to see how many miles they'd drifted left or right in the last few hours groping their way through the murky depths. To their usual astonishment, they found they were only fifty meters off course. The truck and headlights were to their immediate right.

"What's your dive team number?!" the instructor yelled. Exhausted and cramped, Cory straightened out his ankles and back, quickly readjusting to the above-surface world. It was like being born all over again into a world of sight, sounds, and gravity. They ran down the beach back to the assembly area glad to be able to finally breathe again.

* * *

Sitting in his office, surrounded by the photos and ribbons, Cory smiles to himself. He remembers all the years after, too. He reflects on Jumpmaster school, Air Assault school, demolition ranges, weapons training, PT in the mornings, airborne jumps in the afternoon. He remembers the vehicle maintenance, team equipment inventory days, and standing in a thousand formations. They had ceremonies and occasions commemorating just about everything throughout the years.

From time to time, he would think of his dad too. It really never made sense to him. After his death, Robert McGuire was quickly and unceremoniously cremated. The train that struck him mutilated and dragged his body for miles before finally spitting him out on the side of the tracks. Never taking the opportunity to fully process the tragedy, Cory just went on staying busy and living his life.

Everything revolved around the many deployments,

specifically deployments to train and work with other country's military special operations units. Deployments to Pakistan and deep into the country near the Kashmir region; into Kenya and several hour's drive from Nairobi; Yemen over the mountains near the Red Sea; Oman conducting airborne jumps into the Arabian Sea; small boat operations and desert operations in places like Qatar and Kuwait.

Repeatedly, he went overseas. Months and months were spent in difficult and dangerous environments. Eight months a year, he was somewhere other than home.

CHAPTER TWENTY-SIX

Cory glances at the Purple Heart award hanging on the wall and next to it a picture of him and a newly promoted Sergeant Major Trotten. He remembers his first combat deployment and almost reflexively, he rubs his right hand.

* * *

It was May 2004 around 1000-hours on the far side of Mosul, Iraq where Cory's team was mounting a convoy from their patrol base. It was a clear day and the air was a comfortable spring temperature. He was several hundred feet away on the firing range assisting with training.

Even though he was busy, he realized something was wrong. He had a sense of foreboding. At the same time Cory was thinking those thoughts, he started asking questions of the men around him. Cory wanted to know where everyone was? Why were he and just a few soldiers left down on the range?

"The team's mounting a convoy to take the returning team back to Diamondback," he was told.

Cory's heart suddenly jumped – a sudden sense of urgency and duty to be present next to his fellow soldiers. He felt drawn to go and instinctively ran up the dirt bank to find several vehicles waiting. It was a sense of responsibility; a need to help protect. After all, Cory had arrived a few weeks before the rest of his team and he knew the area. Busying themselves around the vehicles, he approached the convoy and heard motors running, radio checks, and voices ordering last minute instructions. It seemed like quick, last minute necessary chaos occurring.

Cory's excitement turned to horror when he found himself staring at the co-driver's side and right front seat of a light-skinned Humvee without armor protection. Given last minute permission to go, this was his vehicle. He was shocked the vehicle was even part of the vehicle convoy.

Out of several military vehicles, it stuck out like a sore thumb. It was a vehicle without an armored turret, bullet proof glass, or three-inch-thick armor reinforcement. It shouldn't go and he knew it. It was too late to do anything about it. He had not said anything in time. He had not gotten there early enough to influence a better decision. Everyone was practically rolling out the front gate. Cory swallowed hard and took the seat. His teammates were already in the vehicle.

Mike was driving. Pete, who was Cory's junior, was standing in the hole that was supposed to be a turret. Then Andy, another long-time team member showed up. He walked up and took a seat, opting not to sit inside but jumping in the back-left corner of the Humvee bed. The atmosphere in the vehicle seemed tense and Cory thought everyone must have felt uncomfortable about the Humvee situation. As soldiers, they accepted their orders, carried them out, and kept their concerns quiet. If anything, they'd attempt to promote confidence to help the situation.

"I love you guys," Cory yelled over the loud engine and fan motor to try and break the tension.

But there was too much invisible anxiety to illicit any reaction. Everyone just kept their thoughts to themselves, trying to concentrate through the situation.

Before they knew it, the lead vehicle had started to pull forward. Sandwiched in the middle were Cory and his Humvee. He steeled himself, settling into his seat. Cory occupied himself by checking systems, adjusting his equipment, and keeping aware of his handheld GPS location. Well on their way, the line of vehicles made their way to and through the front gate. Moving outside the "wire" was a definite point of demarcation, feeling like the point of no return.

Cory took one last look at their pathetic situation. Internally he felt devastated. Windows were down, the sheet metal doors jingled, and Pete stood in his hole holding an M-4 assault rifle. Where there should have been an armored turret and machine gun there was only Pete standing completely exposed. Andy sat in the back in a bench seat, also exposed. Cory tried to yell at Pete to come down. Pete couldn't hear him, so Cory yelled louder over the roar of the motor. Still no reaction. Either Pete didn't hear him, or he was just too brave not to stay there.

The convoy snaked down the hill, taking a right onto the deserted boulevard. The typical Iraqi urban setting took shape. Abandoned stores, mud huts, and rusting fences lined the streets. Arabic language billboards and shop fronts gave color to the otherwise dry, dusty debris-strewn city. The convoy made a U-turn crossing through a three-foot-high median. They were finally on their way to the on-ramp of the highway where they would travel fast toward Diamondback.

A fifteen-foot-high plaster wall sat off to the right side and gently curved. Everyone wore helmets, eye protection, armor plated vests and had their weapons in a ready state to react to any immediate threats. They had left the first phase of danger behind. Before them though, was an on-ramp of sorts with a curve to negotiate. Cory used his arm to keep him and his extra weight from falling toward the driver's side while they kept veering sharply right. He was glad the window was down too. He'd anticipated what a whole panel of glass might feel like if it suddenly exploded into his face. Cory took one last look at the wall, then to his front again.

He was suddenly slammed on his right side by a huge explosion, but felt submerged, swimming and spinning as if caught in a giant wave. There was no sight or sound, only darkness.

He floated but was completely aware of where he was and why. Somehow, he knew the submersion would end and he'd be brought back to the surface. Strangely, it was not terror-inducing but oddly peaceful.

Then he was back, staring at the blackened deformed windshield. The Humvee was bumping and weaving in a cloud of smoke, debris and heat.

Cory looked at Mike who was too busy still driving to spare him a return glance. Mike was trying to get them to safety after what had been a sudden IED to the right side of the vehicle. He felt like everything was in a slow motion and nothing seemed real. There was no sound except for a high-pitched ringing in his ears.

Though extremely muffled, he could hear Pete scream out in pain and the radio blare, "We're hit! We're hit!"

Parts of Cory's body started to burn and ache, and his entire right arm was numb. He wasn't even sure if he still had it. For a moment, he almost smiled at the irony. He couldn't believe that they'd been blown up. That *he'd* gotten blown up. First time out.

He started a mental inventory of his body from top to bottom.

Mike had raced the disabled and smoldering Humvee a hundred meters to a stop. Others were already out of their vehicles and running by when someone came and motioned for Mike to get out and run to a nearby position to pull security.

Men pulled Pete out of the turret position. He was in obvious and extreme pain. Cory found himself alone. He took his helmet off and dropped it. Looking around, he could see they had all pulled off the on-ramp and onto an adjacent road. Everyone was pulling security in different directions.

The right side of Cory's vehicle was severely damaged. Most likely, two 81mm mortars were taped together and packed with bolts and nails for extra shrapnel effect. He knew about them— they all knew about them. The metal projectiles couldn't have been ten feet away when they exploded into Cory and his side of the vehicle. He felt like someone had hit him in the side of the face with a bat and he could smell burnt hair. It was hard to see out the windows, make out what was happening, or know where they were exactly.

He tried to reach the door handle to get out but couldn't. He felt as if he was half-paralyzed with a double force of gravity pushing down on him. He was so tired, more tired than he'd ever been.

Cory ran the hand he could feel over his chest, legs, and down to his feet. Apprehensively, he checked his face. He was relieved when it felt like it was still in one piece. Blood was dripping, but he couldn't tell from where. Finally, Cory looked at his right arm. To his surprise, it was there. However, at his elbow, an entire section of uniform was ripped out and blood was pumping out like a tipped over oil can. An entire chunk of Cory's right elbow had been blown away by the blast. Two inches of his brachial artery were gone.

Before Mike could even get the Humvee through the kill zone to a safe stop, Cory had already lost the critical pressure and blood volume to function. He was going to bleed out. He tried to reach his wounded arm with his other but for some reason, it wasn't possible. He wanted to cut off the blood flow. He looked around and tried to call for help, but even his voice was too weak to carry. Cory realized he'd probably die right there within a matter of a few minutes.

He raised his arm up onto the window sill to elevate and slow the flow of blood. With that, he could hear the team working on Pete and it sounded like things were as bad as they could get. In fact, Pete had been hit in his ear just under the helmet by a large piece of shrapnel that penetrated deep. Cory leaned back, hoping he could relax his breathing and pulse to slow the loss of blood. Just then, a teammate ran by asking him if he was okay.

Cory wanted to say "Yes. And . . .," but all he could manage to get out was, "Yes." And just like that his help was gone. He tried to think full sentences but couldn't. He tried to pray but found that was also impossible. All his thoughts just seemed to end.

Suddenly, Cory's heart skipped a beat and it labored to find a new rhythm. His breathing was shallow and difficult. He was doing everything he could to stay awake, but it was no use.

Oh no. Not yet. He realized that dying wasn't painful or scary. And there was no pain or sadness because his mind was merely drifting away. He was so tired . . ..

Just before his eyes closed, he watched the smoky, cracked and deformed Humvee windshield fade away.

CHAPTER TWENTY-SEVEN

"Cory? Cory?"

It seemed like many hours had passed, but it was probably only minutes or seconds when Cory opened his eyes to see who was calling his name. He swiveled his head slightly to see the team medic bent over at the door's window. The medic said a few more words and Cory nodded in agreement.

Like a man trying to survive a journey through the desert with no water, he was mentally exhausted. The medic ran his hands around his head, behind his back, then down and around his legs, quickly checking for more serious wounds.

Breathing heavy and sweating profusely, the medic pulled a nylon tourniquet out of his kit and turned it tight, then tighter around Cory's right arm. Cory knew it was necessary pain, but the pressure was killer. Like a water faucet shut off, the bright red flow stopped.

Cory tried to speak but couldn't say more than two words of any significance. The medic told Cory he would be back and then ran away, out of sight. Again, Cory was alone with his thoughts.

He struggled with the fact that they'd been hit. He wondered who hit them? From where? Who else was wounded or killed? As his thoughts carried on, the pain on the right side of his face began to escalate. Simultaneously, he marveled at the complete lack of feeling in his right hand and arm.

His gaze drifted to the floor. On the floorboards he noticed a pool of blood filling the entire floor pan. He saw the jagged holes where shrapnel had penetrated. He thought the whole right front side of the vehicle must have been shredded and torn.

The medic returned with a few more teammates to recover Cory from the Humvee. They pulled him up, then out of the seat. Cory put his left arm around one of his teammate's shoulders and together they half-carried him to another Humvee. Just like that, he'd escaped his coffin and isolation and was headed into the light. They placed him hurriedly in the back seat, but he noticed their looks of concern.

He tried to lighten the mood for them–they didn't need to be worried about him. He mumbled that corny old movie line, "Tell my wife and kids I love them."

Unfortunately, he was unable to apply the necessary humorous connotation to it.

With every additional word he attempted, he realized he couldn't make his brain function.

* * *

Cory and Pete were transported to a small, nearby medical facility. Luckily it was less than a ten-minute drive but seemed like an eternity.

The Marine Corps-style Quonset hut sat on the corner of a small military outpost, nestled in the middle of a walled and secured section of some former Iraqi government-type base with a US presence and security.

Cory was pulled from the back seat and carried toward the

tent with a red cross painted on it. The tents were semi-structures in that they had doors and windows and some sectional walls and flooring. A medic in scrubs waited at the door already wearing surgical gloves. Through the swinging doors, Cory found a whole new level of intensity. The orderlies, nurses, medics, and doctors moved with a purpose. An entire team of medical staff grabbed him. Questions were rapid fire.

"Blood type?"

"Where have you been hit?"

"What happened?"

"Can you feel that?"

Holding Cory's right arm, the doctor touched different spots on his hand and arm. Cory couldn't feel anything. They asked him to move his fingers. With all his might, he couldn't make the slightest movement.

He was lifted onto a table. They cut his boots, trousers and shirt off, and then piled his body armor and helmet on top of it all in a stack in a corner. A light blue hospital gown was put on him. Five people at once were ramming in IVs, inserting catheters, and flashing lights in his eyes and ears.

Cory's right side felt heavy, like a thousand pounds of pain and discomfort. The catheter was the biggest surprise and hurt more than he ever thought possible. Though he'd only been there three to five minutes he couldn't understand why so much hospital prep was being done in some tent.

As he lay there, Cory could hear Pete being prepped too. Looking over, he could see his arms and legs in constant motion like he was in terrible pain. Cory listened to him moan and knew Pete was hurt bad. Real bad.

Then the doctor started calling off to the team what he was seeing on Cory. "Right temporal lobe penetration, left hypothalamus, lower cranial, soft tissue, tympanic, nasal cavity pressure and metal frag, fluids unremarkable, burn, right side face and hair, open right shoulder, graze, brachial separation and tissue, paralysis, left leg undetermined penetration, left top foot chemical or fragment, third degree."

Nothing Cory wanted to say would offer much assistance. His ability to communicate seemed to be gone. He wanted to know how Pete was doing. And where was the team? Where were they going and when? The medical team rewrapped Cory's gaping wound and in addition, bandaged his neck, side of head, and his left leg and foot.

Cory just lay there wearing the clear rubber oxygen mask. He scanned the operating room atmosphere and noticed the bloody gloves and gauze laying everywhere. His ears still rung loudly and the sounds around him were muffled. In his own strange world, he thought about how different life was just twenty minutes ago. He was no longer an armor-wearing warrior but now a soot-faced, bloody, hospital-gowned casualty. He couldn't hear much or speak at all. He couldn't even keep a thought straight.

He was a casualty staring at his pile of combat equipment while listening to the muffled cries of his buddy.

* * *

The doctors administered sedatives and the medevac helicopter swooped onto the pad just before dark. Cory looked at the compartment side-doors slide open and noticed only darkness. The force of the wind and the wop wop wop of the blades were uncomfortable, but he didn't have much pain. Maybe the worst thought of all was that he couldn't even defend himself, let alone anyone else. Now he was just a piece of damaged Army equipment that needed to be quickly transported back to FOB

Diamondback.

As the dust flew from the rotor wash, the hands of a medic leaned over Cory to shield him until he got to the point of loading. Then four soldiers ran the stretcher out to the awaiting helo and slid him into one of the four stretcher rows. Cory felt like his nose was scraping the bottom of whatever was just above him. Then the claustrophobia set in. He couldn't see or hear anything, just the wop, wop, wop. Cory laid in his slot vibrating and rocking to the idling medevac. Time went on and he waited for something, anything to happen.

Finally, with darkness all around him, Cory could see figures at his feet loading someone above him. It was Pete. Once they were secured in their "bunks" the helicopter rapidly powered up and lifted, banking hard to clear enemy fire.

Even as a kid enduring his father's violent, drunken tirades chasing them from the house, Cory hadn't felt so vulnerable, weak and scared as he did there flat on his back in the pitch-black helicopter. He'd envisioned the helo ride differently; more like him and Pete side by side on a big floor where a buddy and medic kept them company, like in the movies.

But no, this was an airborne local bus that made more stops, loaded more wounded, and leapfrogged their way finally to FOB Diamondback.

* * *

Cory awoke to his company commander, team sergeant and the unit's chief warrant officer standing over him. Looking up, he saw them huddled over him like doctors observing a patient. Cory couldn't make sense of where he was or why. All he knew was it was time to get up.

He said, "Let's go," but somehow, he didn't. Then he whispered, "I need to find..." But he couldn't get his body to do what he wanted it to do.

"Just hang in there and lie back down, Soldier," his CO told him with a pat on the shoulder.

Recognizing his disorientation, the warrant officer, a former medic, got down eye to eye with Cory.

"You guys got hit. You're back at Diamondback. We got you."

With that, Cory went unconscious again.

CHAPTER TWENTY-EIGHT

As if a moment later, Cory woke again. He'd been flown by medevac an hour away to COB Speicher in Tikrit. This time, an entire surgical team wearing masks encircled him.

"What is your blood type?" the surgeon asked.

Cory answered in a barely audible whisper. "Where am I?" he whispered.

Instantly annoyed, the Army doctor said, "You're in the combat support hospital in Tikrit. Just relax."

The team wanted to get to work and they put an oxygen mask on Cory. With his eyes closed, Cory heard the nurse giving him what was supposed to be subconscious information, designed to help a patient tolerate procedures by telling them what they were doing while the patient was under general anesthetic.

Unfortunately, Cory thought she was just being kind–the nurse thought he was completely sedated. He felt the metal bars pry open his mouth and slip over his tongue. She told him to relax and not swallow.

Cory figured out they were trying to open his throat and insert a breathing tube. The nurse continued her instruction. Cory tried to relax knowing that what he was experiencing was a medical requirement, but he knew something was wrong. She fed the tube down alongside the cold steel. Cory accommodated her by opening his throat as wide as he could. Then it happened.

The tube made it extremely difficult to breathe around. Cory fought to get air around the tube that blocked his efforts.

The nurse sounded angry. "Relax. Don't breathe around it. Let it breathe for you."

He didn't understand. Let *what* breathe for him? When? How?

The nurse told the surgeon, "he's breathing around it," as though she didn't know he was awake. Then Cory understood the circumstances. He wasn't supposed to be awake.

The surgeon replied, "Pump the ball all the way up."

Cory knew exactly what that meant. And it meant that what little air he was getting would be completely blocked off.

Pumping the ball, the nurse kept up her mantra: "Stop fighting it. Let the machine breathe for you."

Cory felt the hose expand completely and the promised air didn't fill his lungs. Total panic set in and Cory started convulsing. He tried to get away from her, to pull the tube out, but his wrists were strapped, and the team was holding him down.

"Put him under!" voices screamed in unison.

Cory flailed, frantically trying to get air.

"He's awake. Put him under!" the doctor ordered someone.

Cory's body heaved, and his legs kicked as he waited for the madness to end. His body was responding to the panic and lack of oxygen, but his mind was counting on the team to properly sedate him.

* * *

Next time, Cory woke up in a hospital recovery room and air was rhythmically and steadily being pushed into his lungs through the tube. He felt the air go in perfectly and thought, "Oh. So, that's what it feels like."

Fully awake, he managed to swallow around the tube. He wanted it out. He wanted it out *immediately*. He felt stupid having a machine breathe for him when he could do that himself.

Whenever the orderly or nurses came in his room, he motioned for them to remove the tube. Slowly they inched the tube out of his lung cavity until at last he was free of the tube and the breathing apparatus. Looking himself over in the light of day, he seemed covered in bruises.

When Cory was able, in a raspy voice he asked, "Where am I now?"

"You're in Baghdad. And the two of you will be going to Rhein-Main near Frankfurt, Germany shortly."

Cory looked across the room and saw Pete propped up in his bed. Cory immediately noticed the breathing tube and how Pete was scratching and pulling at it. Cory knew Pete wanted it out—he could read his body language. So, he tried to talk whoever came in the room to take Pete off the machine. After all, they did it for him, right?

Once again, they relented. Pete coughed up the long tube. He must have originally put on a good act, but it wasn't long before the nurses had to reinsert the tube.

Something wasn't right about how Pete was acting. He was awake and aware one minute, then he drifted into states of varying consciousness. For the most part, the medical team wanted to believe he was just tired or that it was just his personality. No one understood the small hole penetrating Pete's right ear was so serious or that he could have brain damage.

But Pete had been wounded just eight months prior in Al Ramadi while they were clearing a house of insurgents and his body was more susceptible to infection. He'd been shot in the calf muscle of his left leg, but it was a through and through wound, meaning the bullet had entered and exited without hitting any bone. Cory's friend, who was Pete's team sergeant, and a medic on another team were killed. Cory wondered if that injury had anything to do with what Pete was experiencing now.

While Cory contemplated that, Pete was transported to Germany, leaving Cory to worry about his friend. While he hated being separated from him, Cory couldn't really be much help to him, either.

When it was Cory's turn to move to Germany, he was wheeled to the front doors of the hospital and waited with a few familiar faces to see him off.

Assigned as liaisons in Baghdad, Cory's old sergeant major and company commander made small talk with him, never mentioning the burned hair or his face, blackened and dirty from the blast. When it was time, they escorted his gurney out to the helicopter. They helped load him, then waved goodbye as the chopper lifted off. Cory was flown to the nearby air base where he was then loaded onto a plane headed for Germany.

Another leg of the long, long journey.

* * *

Descending from the clouds, his transport landed at Rhein-Main Air Base where it was rainy, cool, and green. He was taken by ambulance to another hospital.

This time, Cory and Pete were in separate rooms. He couldn't see Pete, but he could feel his presence. It was a certain heaviness he could sense but he couldn't quite put his finger on.

An older, distinguished surgeon came into Cory's room and

told him a delicate procedure would be required to remove a large nail head from the back of his skull. The shrapnel had stopped just millimeters from his spinal cord at the brain stem and was crimping off the flow of the cerebral artery that supplied blood to his brain and blood vessels. If the object was left in place and then jolted or moved in any way, it could sever the artery.

Cory understood and agreed to the surgery. Dead was not better than being paralyzed, so without further discussion, Cory prepared himself for the unknown.

* * *

For the fourth or fifth time in two weeks, Cory was put under general anesthesia and woke to unfamiliar surroundings and confusing circumstances. Again, he went through the routine of tubes and breathing machines.

While in recovery, a visiting doctor noticed Cory's dirty and unshaven face. He approached the bed and smiled.

"We can't let you go home looking like this, now can we?"

The doctor shaved and cleaned Cory's face. Not long after that, more gauze bandages were applied to the new four-inch incision at the back of his head and neck. Soon they would place Cory into another ambulance to make his way to another waiting Air Force plane.

As he was being wheeled out, his surgeon came alongside and handed him a small sealed plastic cup.

"Thought you might like to have the thing that almost got you," he said.

Cory took the cup and looking inside it, saw a quarter-inch-diameter nail head. As he exhaled a long sigh he stared at it, slowly shaking his head.

CHAPTER TWENTY-NINE

Finally, en route to the States and Dover Air Force Base in Washington D.C., it seemed like Cory had the medical C-5 airplane all to himself. Although there were countless two and three-bed high patient stretchers throughout, he was the only patient. Everyone else was returning medical personnel rotating out and back to the US.

On a bottom row, somewhere in the middle of the maze of stretchers, Cory laid with an I.V. hanging above his head. Except for his assigned nurse, not many others paid him much attention. Their minds were on home. They were excited and energized about finally being able to leave another deployment behind. There was laughing and joking, loud talking and fun conversation all around him.

But Cory was in another place, a different frame of mind. And he was starting to feel small and insignificant–out of place. He asked for a sedative or pain medicine so he could escape the loneliness for a while. He closed his eyes and listened to the low roar of the wind and engines, wondering how Pete and his family were doing. Pete was on his mind when the medication and engine drone lulled him to sleep.

At two in the morning there wasn't much activity at the end of the taxi way. It was dark with no sound but that of jet engines powering down. The tail ramp was down, and Cory lay on a stretcher watching all the others talk among themselves as they deplaned and boarded a shuttle bus.

At first, he was alone in the middle of the runway with an attendant. Then a man drove up in a vehicle and approached Cory. He draped a patriotic blanket across his chest and then saluted.

"On behalf of a grateful nation, thank you for your honor and sacrifice."

In the middle of the night, in the dark, on a deserted tarmac, Cory listened to the words the soldier had probably recited a hundred times before. Then he helped load Cory into the ambulance that had pulled quietly alongside them.

That was his homecoming. He was reminded of the last time his father had left him standing at the airport, ignored and insignificant. As they buckled down his gurney, he felt just a little bit smaller.

* * *

At Walter Reed Hospital in the Intensive Care Unit, Cory woke up to a half-lit room, monitors beeping and IV lines dripping. There was a smell of a sour, poorly sanitized room. It was like an outdated hospital environment where one could imagine a wounded soldier lying there continuously since WWII.

The sheets were old and thin. A light blue bed cover brought zero comfort. It was cold, and Cory felt helpless and alone. His arm was re-bandaged and rested across his chest. His face felt like it had just left the battlefield. His sinus passages were clogged with congealed blood and mucus. People walked by the door but moved too quickly and never saw Cory waving his hand for help.

He looked around and wondered where Pete was. He knew he was in the same hospital somewhere. He could feel him. Cory wondered about the team, too. He imagined that he had let them down. He wished he was back there but, at the same time, he was glad he wasn't. A team was only as good as its weakest link. Cory didn't want to get anyone else hurt.

Before he could think too many more thoughts, a nurse came rushing in to prep him for yet another surgery. The intercom called out for something else needed for somewhere else. Cory was an item, and Walter Reed a resource, a machine for getting items working again.

* * *

Three days after his third surgery, Cory woke to find an old friend sitting beside his bed, a magazine in his hands and a cup of steaming coffee on the table.

"Well, I'm glad to see you got some shut eye," Trotten said with a smile. "Stinkin' bad luck, Seventy-six. Is there anything I can do for you, since you don't look like you'll be throwing on a ruck any time soon?"

Cory smiled at the man who'd been such a positive influence for him through his training years and beyond.

"No Sergeant Major, but it's really good to see you. Gets a bit hard laying here waiting to get better."

Trotten nodded. "Worse than any other kind of waiting, isn't it?"

"How long can you stay?" Cory asked, hoping he'd have some company for a few days, anyway.

"I fly out tomorrow morning, but I'll stop in on my way back next week. And bein' you're so full of holes and whatnot now, I'm gonna have to take care of you until you stop leaking. Since I never had any, you're like a son to me, you know."

Cory thought about that. "I do. Thank you. You have helped me more than you will ever know," he replied.

The two men sat in silence for several minutes. "The nurse said you've been dreaming a lot. Been mumbling about your dad, Detroit, and things. You want to finally tell me about your father's accident? I never pressed you about it, and maybe you never thought I needed to hear about it," Trotten said.

"I never tell anyone about it. It was pretty strange, really," Cory began. "Sometimes, when I think about it, which isn't too often anymore, I'm not sure it was real. I mean, the train did quite a number on him and they couldn't do a proper identification, really. The height, weight and build seemed to fit, though. He was wearing the new raincoat I'd sent him for Christmas the year before. And his wallet mostly survived being in his back pocket, but it was hard for me to think my father would kill himself. He was many things, but he wasn't the type to do that."

Trotten seemed to consider that. "Maybe he was a hero after all, Cory. Maybe he thought the way to help you was to set you free." He cleared his throat. "I'm not saying it was the right thing to do, but you said he drank a lot. Sometimes the logic is affected, you know? People do all kinds of things when they love somebody."

"I know," Cory said. "But at the funeral, I talked to Mr. Kennedy who ran an alcohol center in the area and he said my father was sober. Funny, no matter how I tried, I couldn't remember him sober, ever. Sad that I didn't get that chance. My sister either. She's older than I am, and she never knew him any way but drunk and mean. Anyway, we had his remains interred at the National Cemetery. I'll bet the only really happy days he had were when he was in the Army. He was the reason I wanted to serve so badly."

"I remember," Trotten said with a nod. "How about now? When you get cleared, you going back to an A-team?"

"I hope so. If I can, I will. My sister is after me to figure out my life after I get out, but I'm not ready for that. I hope this isn't the end of the road for me. I spent a lot of time getting here. Get taken out for good after only two weeks? This story can't end this way. I have got to keep going and see what's around the next bend. There has got to be more to this story."

Trotten shakes his head. "I know, Seventy-six. I know your heart. Drive on with that mission then. You're not out of the picture yet. You've got a lot of work ahead of you to recover, but you're going to be back, going down range. I'm sure of it."

The nurse came in with medication and reluctantly, Cory took the pills. "Thanks for coming to see me, Sergeant Major. I appreciate it more than I can tell you right now."

"You bet, Cory. You're a good man and a fine Green Beret. You know I'm proud to know you."

With a left-handed handshake, Trotten gave him a nod and was out the door. Finally, Cory laid his head down and allowed the tears to fill his eyes.

* * *

After two weeks, Cory could visit Pete again who was one floor above him in a long-term ward.

Pete's parents, like Cory's, were already passed on, but Cory was delighted to meet Pete's wife and sisters and immediately went into the mode of trying to help them all. It gave him some focus, some purpose for waking up each morning.

The worry and frustration on their faces touched him deeply.

Just like in Germany, no one seemed to know why Pete wasn't getting any better. He looked bad. Cory tried to be an advocate of sorts, stepping in to get better care for Pete or, at least, some answers. The injury to his head made it hard for Pete to communicate clearly and because he had a tube coming out of his windpipe, he couldn't verbalize anything. When he wanted to communicate, he had to write it down.

Sometimes it was hard for any of them to understand what he needed or how he truly felt and that hurt Cory most of all. To make matters worse, the doctors weren't providing much information or any real prognosis.

Cory understood that the busy ward was understaffed and that getting any quality personal medical attention was almost impossible. They rarely saw the same doctor twice; most of the doctors were doing some form of residency.

The bottom line was that Pete wasn't getting better.

* * *

Though his energy was limited, Cory tried to help. If nothing else, he hoped to be an encouraging friend to Pete and his family. As Trotten had for him, Cory longed to make sure that Pete knew how valuable and appreciated he was.

Eight days later it was time for Cory to be discharged from Walter Reed and sent to his home base hospital for continuing care.

After sharing a smile and handshake with Pete, Cory gave everyone in the family a hug and said goodbye. As he walked down the hall for the last time, tears welled in his eyes because he felt like he was abandoning his friend at the worst possible time. But there was nothing else he could do; once again he and Pete would be separated.

He hoped they'd be able to reconnect again once Pete arrived back at the hospital in Fort Campbell.

Regardless, he knew he had to get better, too. Things were what they were. It was time to leave: he'd survived Walter Reed.

* * *

Cory returned home and to the hospital at Fort Campbell where they prepared him to start recovering with bed-rest and medications. There were x-rays, rehabilitation, constant tests and follow-up appointments to keep.

Most of his unit was still deployed, so he was on his own to get through whatever recovery he could. Cory worried about Pete and often called his wife and sisters for updates only to find that things were not getting better.

Cory had his own problems, as it seemed he was getting lost in the medical system, too. Every doctor or provider had to be told repeatedly why he was there, what his injuries were, what had happened, and what was currently ailing him.

He was on ten different medications including antibiotics, nerve pills, stool softeners, and various pain relievers. He had to sleep on his back with his arm and leg elevated, careful to keep the right side of his head from touching the pillow. Every wound oozed and throbbed and swelled.

He woke up in cold sweats. His legs ran every night as though he was running away from something. He woke up gasping for breath like he was suffocating. Because of the trauma to the right side of his head and the destruction of his eardrum and damaged inner ear, the room spun all the time.

Every time he moved, the room spun more and more until he was forced to throw up into a bucket on the side of the bed. Lying in bed for hours on end, he stared at his heavily-bandaged right arm. He endured waves of burning and aching pain, but no other feeling in his hand or arm. His hand and fingers were totally paralyzed. He wondered if he'd ever be able to use his damaged arm again.

At long last, a doctor performed a nerve conduction test on Cory's arm. He applied electric leads to different muscles from his fingers all the way up to the top of his arm. A microphone made crackling sounds when the doctor touched each spot with a probe.

Cory noticed how the doctor shook his head over and over as he listened to the intensified crackling sound. The test revealed that Cory's nerves had been severely damaged or even severed entirely.

The doctor politely told him that his hand had very little chance of improving. Cory returned home, dead arm and all, completely demoralized, though when his sister called to check on him, he refused to let her know the truth about the extent of his injuries.

"Getting better every day, Sis, don't worry," he assured her.

During the long nights he gained a better understanding of what his father might have suffered before stepping onto those tracks. Hopelessness? Fear of being useless for the rest of his life? Cory was determined to find a better way, a way to heal and get back to what he was trained to do.

He'd been home almost three months when the team sergeant in Iraq called and asked him to come back to help them out.

Over seventy-five-hundred miles away, the sergeant had no idea what Cory's condition was, and no one had thought to keep the chain of command posted.

Cory explained that the doctors wouldn't release him yet. It was one of the hardest things he'd ever done.

CHAPTER THIRTY

It was approximately thirty days after that call when Cory got the word that another incident occurred in Iraq and another of his unit members had become a casualty. The major, who was the commander of Company D, had been killed by a mortar attack.

They were returning his body to the States to be buried in Arlington National Cemetery. Cory requested permission to attend the service and permission was granted. He also saw the trip as an opportunity to see Pete at nearby Walter Reed.

Cory still needed help getting dressed. With one hand, he couldn't button his buttons or lace and tie his boots. He had just enough energy to make the trip and attend the funeral.

After the service, Cory made his way to Walter Reed and found Pete still in his hospital bed. His wife was by his side and it didn't look like much had changed. What was obvious to Cory was that Pete looked gaunt, grey, and totally lethargic.

Cory was instantly confused because the doctors talked as though Pete was getting better, but he looked far worse. He was scheduled for a routine surgery to stimulate a damaged nerve in his face.

As Cory sat at the bedside of Pete, he realized how much they had bonded since the IED explosion. They were intimately connected by their shared experience. Cory knew he was the only one in the room that Pete could truly identify with. There was no greater bond than one created by sharing a battle for life and death together.

Cory held back his tears careful not to ruin Pete's obvious optimism. Maybe Pete thought he was on the road to recovery, but it was clear to Cory that he wasn't. Because the doctors needed to prep Pete for the surgery Cory's visit was brief, but he promised to stop by the next day to visit again. They shared a look and a handshake and said goodbye one more time. Cory hugged Pete's wife and told her not to worry, and then, exhausted, dragged himself back to the hotel.

At two in the morning, Cory was awakened by a knock on his hotel room door. He opened the door to find one of the soldiers in charge of their trip standing there. His expression was all business.

"Pete died. He didn't make it through the surgery. His wife wanted you to know she would like you to be part of the funeral."

Two weeks later, Cory delivered a eulogy and helped carry the casket of his friend to its final resting place.

* * *

Through misty eyes, Cory scans the framed newspaper article he kept from those days. It includes a picture of him and his team carrying Pete's flag-draped casket.

Rising, he moves to the bookshelf and pulls down a leather-bound scrapbook of sorts. He remembers most of the words but needs to see them all. Pete's funeral remains one of the hardest days in Cory's memory.

He settles back in his chair and thumbs through the pages

looking for the eulogy he worked on for hours. He finds it and begins to read.

It is an honor and privilege to be standing here today representing the ODA and the Special Forces community and to be a witness of my brother Pete; to give an account of the man I saw and experienced. When we're put in the worst of circumstances, people get to see who we truly are and what we're capable of.

Special Forces Assessment and Selection attempts to choose its soldiers based on this idea. When they make conditions the worst for us, they see who we truly are. I can personally confirm for you today that, in Pete, they truly found the best of the best - Honorable, trustworthy, brave, courageous, and with an unshakable faith no matter what the circumstances.

Pete deployed on the second of his last missions for his country. We were part of a mission that would bring us through some potential enemy territory. The mission was simple but dangerous. And what really stuck with me that day was Pete's own distinct kind of bravery and courage. You can always feel that sort of thing with people, but Pete seemed to have a whole lot extra. He was all about the mission. Even though he had been tried by fire many times before being wounded less than a year prior, he was not hesitant in the least. Instinctively, he took the most dangerous position in the least defendable vehicle. Pete stood in the open turret strong and confident. He was ready for anything. Just by him being there, it seemed to help me be brave.

It wasn't long after we hit the streets that an IED was

initiated directly onto our vehicle with catastrophic results.

I was wounded, and I know Pete was too. I could hear him. But Pete came to my aid with his unspoken bravery and courage. You see, Pete didn't cry or panic, scream or weep, he just sounded angry. It was as if he was trying to shake it off and get back to the mission.

In the next few months, as I began my own recovery, I had the opportunity to visit Pete numerous times. And once again, it was Pete who was doing the inspiring. But it was this last of final missions for his country that Pete brought bravery, courage and honor to a whole new level. You see, I think in Pete's heart of hearts he knew that he was dying. Yet he spent all his energy being strong for us and helping us along. He lasted as long as he could mentally and physically. And then, in his own unique and courageous way, he said goodbye, letting go.

In many of my privileged moments with Pete, from Iraq to Walter Reed Hospital, I told him how proud the team and I were of him, and how much he inspired me to be able to stay the course. He suffered and endured and never complained. To put it simply, he was truly my hero. I was also able to share with him that lives were now being saved because of the sacrifice he made on that fateful day. Army business would be done differently because of what they learned that day. I could tell that really meant a lot to him.

You know, after Pete died, a friend told me that Pete is going to a place that has to be better than here. And when you think about it like that, it must be true. Somehow, we've just gotten used to living under an angry sky and tremoring earth, where sickness, death and suffering are all around us; where misguided people plot to harm good people at every turn.

I know so many of you prayed for Pete, for his recovery, and for God's will to be done. And I think our prayers for Pete were answered and made perfect by Him. He suffers no more. He has suffered enough. You might be asking yourself why people like Pete, good and noble, are wounded and die? I believe it's because our Maker has given us a rare opportunity, a rare gift, for just a splinter of time. The gift of free will - to be like Him, where our choices, our decisions and actions impact all those around us, just so we might know that all things are possible.

You can choose to do good or bad, right or wrong. You can choose to be a fighting soldier who ultimately tries to help relieve the world of evil which seeks only to harm the innocent. Or you can choose to be no one - somebody that does nothing.

Pete chose to help, to render up his body as a living sacrifice so that others might live fully knowing that by going into service in this way he may not live a very long life. But if he was willing, God, our nation, and the world were grateful. Pete knew this and accepted the consequences of his choices. He was willing to sacrifice his life for the betterment of mankind. So that perhaps because of his commitment to this righteous cause, maybe, just maybe, regular citizens all over the world could safely tuck their children into bed knowing someone out there, like Pete, was making that possible. And this will be Pete's legacy - securing the world, making it a safer place where children safely drift off to sleep with hopeful expectations of sweet dreams.

And if you doubt a Creator exists, just look to the heavens, and the vast universe to know it is so. And if you look into your own heart of hearts you know it's true. We are a special creation made by God, living here for a short time so we can impact lives and know what it's like to be like Him.

Pete knew his Maker and had a relationship with Him. But there is always comfort when others want to pray for you. And I saw Pete's hand cover the hand that prayed for him. He was prayed for in the name of Jesus. And he did not push it away or lie rigid in discomfort. Instead, he pulled in, held on, and grasped for his Savior. He was at peace with death long before he passed away. I've never met someone so unafraid of death. Again, Pete continued to inspire me just like he had that day we mounted up for the mission.

I am simply in awe of this young man. And look! He's still inspiring us. Right here, right now. So, when you tuck your children in safe and sound tonight, know that it was Pete who made that possible.

Today we are honoring the life of a true hero. I don't know what else you could call him.

On the cover of my Bible, a piece of scripture reads, "Neglect not the gift that is in thee." Pete was obedient to use his gift of bravery and service to his country. And so, Pete continues to inspire us so that maybe we can do the same.

Thank you, Buddy. I will miss you. But all of us who have established our relationship with God as you have done, we are sure to see you there, that place 'that's got to be better than here.' That perfect place where people suffer no more. And where finally we're able to take rest from our earthly journey. Where our Father will say, 'Well done, my good and faithful servant.'

What else would Pete want to say? "I love you, Caylee, and I love you, Terri and Mindy. You too, Grandma and Grandpa. I will miss you very much, and I know you will miss me. But till then, please live happy, content lives, and use your gift. Whatever it is, use it. And I'll see you soon."

Thank you, Caylee, Terri, and Mindy for allowing me to be part of your lives. May God hold you close and carry you all the days of your lives giving you peace, happiness and nothing but fond memories of Pete.

Pete, I salute you. Thank you for being the man you were, and the saint you've now become.

CHAPTER THIRTY-ONE

Cory closes the book of memories and wipes his eyes with his shirt sleeve. He's known a lot of good men in his years with the Army. He'd only known one Pete, though. He'd been blessed for that friendship. He got to his feet and placed the book back into place.

The room has grown a bit darker as the sun continued its march to the west. He realizes he's lost a lot of time while in the den freely reminiscing. He looks out the window and thinks about all the other times he'd spent in Iraq.

* * *

After the team returned from their eight-month deployment to Mosul, they began immediate preparations to return to Iraq for an upcoming May timeframe. Cory's hand and arm started to regain some movement, although he had to use his other hand to assist with mostly everything.

He couldn't button a button or twist off a bottle cap, but he could compensate fairly well with his other hand. Cory did his best to hide the weakness and worked hard to make his fingers and hand do more and more. Everyone turned a blind eye to the disability. Cory returned to Iraq in May. He went alone, volunteering once again to go as the advance party for the team. Cory went with one working hand and arm. It would take years to regain full use again.

* * *

He thinks about one specific day when he just wanted to survive one more military operation. Cory remembers, like it was yesterday, the mission for that day.

* * *

Through his night vision goggles Cory observed the road ahead. The eerie green illumination combined with the typical middle-eastern surroundings cast ghostly silhouettes. Seen were strands of wadded up concertina wire, and loosely strung barbed wire fences where jagged strips of old plastic bag lined the sides of the road. Large pot holes, some filled and others not, dotted the broken asphalt ahead.

The Humvee rumbled along bumping and rocking. Cory's teammate swerved the vehicle side to side like a slalom skier to go between and around any pot hole that looked threatening. In a blur they passed mud houses, abandoned store fronts, packs of barking dogs, and garbage that seemed to dance on the sides of the road.

The men seated within were dark shadows. The glow from the computer tracking screen reflected its eerie light onto Cory's helmet and small red and green bulbs flickered as indicators of the numerous electronics crowding the interior. Wind swept through the turret gunner's position down into the interior of the vehicle. The gunner stood scanning the road, alternating the 50-caliber machinegun, back and forth, into left and right locked positions.

Cory oversaw an early patrol into the Al Jazeera region.

Jazeera meant desert and the team had increased its presence deep into the vastness. The team brought their five vehicles to the designated intersection, stopped, and waited.

It was 0445 and the friendly Iraqi counterpart force was late. In the moonless predawn, on an isolated stretch of city outskirts like sitting ducks, they waited. Before long, a steady stream of distant headlights was seen. What Cory thought would be ten to fifteen vehicles turned out to be closer to like fifty or more. Obviously, Lt. Ali, the commander in charge of the Iraqi force, thought he'd need extra help that day. Cory and the team's mission was to intercept a high level Al Qaida propaganda ministry meeting taking place in a remote desert village several kilometers away.

Cory would be responsible for Lt. Ali and whomever he brought along. It was Cory who would have to adapt the plan and reorganize personnel to best suit the mission. From the beginning, which should have been roughly seventy-five soldiers, Cory was immediately made aware that he would now be in charge of approximately two hundred. It was a large order and big change, but standing in the dark, leaning over the hood of a Humvee with maps spread-out, Cory knew that in Special Forces, accepting unpredictable situations came with the territory. The policy of US support was always to allow the Iraqi forces to lead the way and "manage" the mission. However, it was the US forces that tactfully encouraged cooperation whereby the job got done with strong US assistance.

Lt. Ali and another one of his blue and white police trucks would lead the way. Cory would be the second in line and the rest behind him. The column of vehicles would stretch out over a half-mile eventually. To avoid detection and the mine-laden road that led out to the desert, Cory and Lt. Ali decided to travel deep into the landscape and parallel the dangerous road until they reached the bridge at Tariq-Tariq Wadi.

Winding slowly and carefully, the long line of vehicles navigated around bushes, sand dunes, rocks, and washouts. The crude vehicle path was visible for only as far as the black-out drive lights would illuminate. Cory carefully followed each turn and surrounding landscape features by utilizing his GPS computer screen.

After an hour or so, Lt. Ali started to stray off course. Cory and his vehicle took over the lead to steer the column back to the asphalt road. Moving cross country, Cory made the vehicle column intersect back at the road two kilometers before the bridge.

A small village sat adjacent to the bridge and was a reliable landmark to confirm their exact location. Powering up the steep embankment, Cory's vehicle scraped up and onto the road. Before long, every vehicle was traveling back on the road. It was a good and bad feeling - Good that all the vehicles had made it, but bad that they were once more again vulnerable to roadside bombs.

The sun was rising over the eastern edge of the desert and an orange haze spanned the horizon. As the dew of a typical morning collected on the vehicle skins, small black birds darted across the sky.

In the distance Cory could see the short hundred-foot, two-lane bridge. Also visible was the village. Wisps of smoke from the coal burning stoves rose into the sky and wandering goats and sheep grazed freely in fields and courtyards.

Lt. Ali and his other vehicle moved in front of Cory's again and as they reached the point where the village was to their immediate right, bullets hit, pinged, and thudded against their vehicles.

"Contact right!" was echoed on the radio, then, "Contact left."

Cory knew instantly that they were under attack. His instinct was to drive quickly through the buzzing enemy fire. The radios were jammed with voices screaming out direction of fire and commands.

"Move, move, go, go, go!"

Both sides of the vehicles were being hit with multiple weapons fire. Cory's vehicle swerved around Ali's and raced over the bridge, hopefully leading the convoy out of the kill zone.

On the other side the paved road ended, and open desert began. Those on the Iraqi radio frequency were having their own emotionally charged exchanges. It was verbal chaos in both English and Arabic.

The concern was greater for the Iraqis in their lighter armored police vehicles. Directly on top of the Tariq-Tariq Wadi Bridge, Cory thought about the explosion that might come. Instead, more intense enemy fire occurred.

Hammer-like thuds against the left and right-side doors pelted them over and over from the wadi and elsewhere. The thick bulletproof windows started spidering with other thuds, ricochets, and zings.

RPGs must be next, Cory thought. From behind, they could hear their teammates returning fire with machineguns. Cory's own gunner returned 50-cal bursts. Large, hot, brass casings rained down, clanging onto the floorboards around their feet. With the first burst their ears rang which muted all sound around them.

Cory's head and eyes vibrated with every trigger pull from above. The small explosions sent concussive waves within the small cab area. Heavier, more direct automatic enemy fire awaited them to the front after they'd crossed the bridge. Sledge hammered thuds hit their windows and steel. They were in a three-sided, u-shaped ambush.

Eight inches from Cory's nose, his windshield absorbed a massive bullet strike. Had it penetrated, the bullet would have gone straight between Cory's eyes. He swallowed hard and took a deep breath.

Not sure if there were snipers or just blistering concentrated fire, Cory didn't spend much time contemplating the matter. To his surprise, no one else came across the bridge behind them. It was just he and Lt. Ali's two vehicles. They were cornered and alone with only Lt. Ali who was completely pinned down. They were sitting ducks. He thought of the RPGs again but pushed the thought away.

Cory attempted to call the others to rally on him, but because of the surprise of the situation everyone either forgot to turn off their radio frequency jamming, or the enemy force was jamming it for them. Either way, with no radio communication, he needed another plan and quick.

He surveyed the battlefield to his front. The desert was flat with ridges and vehicle tracks fingered off in all directions. The tracks all led to a steady incline of elevation. Further ridges beyond leapfrogged each other and staggered off to the horizon.

The well-camouflaged enemy positions could be anywhere and more traps, standard to insurgent techniques, were probably ahead. The personnel behind him probably didn't realize the wall of lead awaiting them on this side of the bridge. Cory ordered his vehicle to turn around and signaled Ali to follow. He had to get the light-skinned Iraqi trucks to safety and out of the range of the RPGs that were sure to be fired any time now. Crossing back across the bridge, Cory motioned everyone to fall back and get on-line in front of the wadi.

Just then he realized the entire Iraqi force was stopped off the side of the road using the cover of the berm. He raced back to them. The Iraqis were hunched down, some under their vehicles, behind the open doors, or hunkered down inside the cabs, still taking harassing fire which was by no means as intense, but still a threat.

Through his interpreter Elvis, nicknamed for his sideburns and sunglasses, Cory organized the men to move into the village and secure it. Then Cory turned around to get back to the team. From two-hundred-meters away he saw the entire team and a few US support vehicles on the other side of the bridge.

An Iraqi vehicle was tipped into the wadi as if they'd attempted to cross. The scene was bizarre. In some ways it was like watching footage from some war movie. The smoke from weapons fire, a Humvee being hit with enemy rounds moving to evade the attack like a target in a carnival shooting gallery, men running chaotically to get into a better position to return fire all as smoke grenades were exploding....

Cory knew exactly what they were experiencing. They were up close and personally experiencing the deadliest location of the kill zone.

Unfortunately, with the jamming he hadn't been able to warn them beforehand. They also got suckered into the bigger ambush and were trapped because vehicles blocked the bridge to return. What seemed like an eternity to analyze took only an instant.

Cory raced his vehicle back into the fight. By getting some vehicles to move forward, Cory and his team's Humvees were all on line in a semi-circle returning fire to whatever direction they faced. Several 50-Cals, M-60 machineguns, M249s and M4s all firing simultaneously was deafening.

The smoke was thick, and they ran ammunition cans to each other to keep up the fire. Cory's vehicle was to the right side of the semi-circle. As it happened, that is where the enemy was most concentrated. On one of the other Humvees accurate fire was placed on the right front door preventing the team member from dismounting to personally engage the enemy.

But others on the team could dismount and took covered positions from around the vehicles and returned fire. Lt. Ali and the other Iraqi vehicle were well behind Cory's Humvee. They tried to dismount their own vehicles but were rappelled by heavy fire leaving them diving to the floorboards.

Cory finally got an idea of where the heaviest concentration of fire was coming from. It was coming from his right front on a ridge approximately seventy-five meters away. At that point he felt a strange numbness and a certain detachment instead of fear. He was frustrated to the point of fury for the lack of radio communications between him and the team. Also gnawing at him was his anticipation of the RPG rounds that would hit them sooner or later. Although Cory couldn't radio his own team, he was able to call outside to all other support elements.

Before his dash back into the fight he'd made radio contact with headquarters and the patrol base. Cory knew the QRF–Quick Reactionary Force–was on its way. That meant several heavily armed gun trucks were coming, but he wasn't sure how long that would take.

Cory felt like he was in charge of every aspect of the battle. Like a construction foreman he had to direct and manage many moving parts quickly and accurately.

The radio constantly called out, "Striker Four Five." That was the call sign for the team, but it was Cory who had to manage the situation.

On separate radios and frequencies, air assets were advising they were "on station" wanting a situation report and guidance. Attack helicopters made runs up and down Tariq-Tariq Wadi firing mini guns, reporting movements and requesting instructions. They banked low overhead and fired rockets at the suspected enemy ridge. It was followed up with more mini gun fire that swept from one side to the other. Sand and dirt shot up as the rounds hit the ground.

Cory was out of the vehicle with a weapon in one hand and a radio mike to his ear with the other. He surveyed the sky like an air traffic controller does with a busy air space. He had to scream over the continuous machinegun fire, jet, and helicopter noise.

As the scene got more intense the pilot of the F-16 was calm and steady. When he keyed his handset, Cory could hear his peaceful place in the sky. When Cory keyed his handset, the fast-mover pilot got an ear full hearing explosions, automatic weapons fire, and men yelling back and forth.

When the pilot heard the seriousness of the situation, he immediately joined the tempo of the fight and came screaming in.

Because of the proximity of the enemy to the team, the pilot had difficulty distinguishing the team's location from that of the enemy. From Cory's vehicle they threw smoke grenades toward the enemy's positions, but the pilot still thought it too "danger close."

Cory noticed something out of the corner of his eye: muzzle flashes off in the distance to his right flank. Enemy forces were out in the desert taking careful aim and firing single shots one after another. Cory couldn't hear the shots coming to tear into his body, but he could count the milliseconds each one would have taken to hit.

It was odd and interesting all at the same time. He could see the rounds being fired at him but the flashes he saw didn't compute. If he couldn't hear them, they didn't seem as real or deadly somehow.

Not having time to contemplate the oddity, Cory's attention was turned to another scene unfolding before his eyes.

CHAPTER THIRTY-TWO

While the situation became increasingly more confusing and intense, Cory got calmer. As he'd learned in SF schools, the body has a way of turning off everything that's unimportant to focus on a single action. Everything slows down, sounds are muffled and yet instincts stay intensely sharp.

Cory wasn't more courageous than anyone else, his survival mechanisms just worked at peak instinctual levels. He was all but deaf except for the ringing in his ears from the prolonged weapons fire.

One of the Iraqi Humvees moved past Cory's front heading toward his right. The vehicle kept moving until it got about fifty meters from where they could position themselves on a knoll that looked directly onto the enemy terrain. They were firing and engaging well beyond Cory's line of sight.

Meanwhile, Cory attempted to get the F-16 to conduct a strike on that general area. He ran over to one of his other Humvees to have them drive to the Iraqi location on the knoll to get them to fall back. By then, the Iraqi turret gunner had run out of ammunition and was standing in his position defiantly unwilling to move.

For some reason, Cory took his attention off the Iraqi Humvee issue and looked to his immediate front. On the arid, flat terrain where many low hills and ridges sat, he found he was suddenly trapped in a nightmare.

As if just for Cory's own viewing, he watched one RPG round, then two, and finally a third, skip and hop in front of him and settle just five meters away. Almost like marbles instead of deadly missiles, they came in and skidded to a halt, each one a little closer than the last.

It was so amazing they'd failed to explode that Cory moved a few feet forward to see what was going on. From there he could see that the RPG rockets had tape wrapped around the safety pin sections. They would never explode that way. It was a standard procedure to tape them in place for extra safety, but in the enemy's haste they forgot to remove the tape and safety pins. That would have armed the rockets for firing.

Cory shouted, "RPGs!" but no one could hear him. He wondered if there would be more.

Again, the attack helicopters' mini guns fired, and Cory's attention was yanked back to the right flank and the situation with the Iraqi Humvee. The RPG problem would have to wait.

The Humvee had roared back to Cory's position, pulled up and slid to a stop along Cory's driver's side door. At the same time the F-16 requested permission to provide a "show of force" maneuver. It was low, close and thunderously fast, but seemed to have no effect on the situation.

All Cory's senses were strained as he watched the jet lift off the deck and dart straight up out of sight. Continuous weapons fire, radio chatter, and yelling in multiple languages assaulted his ears. His eyes burned while he choked on a cocktail of carbon, smoke, and dirt.

The Iraqi men were dragging a limp body down and through the vehicle doors to the ground at the foot of his vehicle. Iraqi soldiers cried and wailed, kneeling, and throwing dirt into the air in mourning. The defiant turret gunner had been shot in the head.

Cory's driver, who was also the team medic, dismounted and started to work on the Iraqi, refusing Cory's offer to help. The Iraqi's friends were drawing attention to their position however, and rounds were being re-directed to their location.

Cory shouted and pointed at the dirt flying up. The medic angrily tried to get the Iraqis to stop their mourning ritual, but they didn't understand. Puffs of dirt and ricochets pinged off the ground and wheel wells. Cory's medic dragged the injured man deeper between the vehicles hoping it would cover and protect them enough.

Cory rushed to the other side of the Humvee feeling the overwhelming need to do something to assist. There he could provide up close communication with the medic, wave off the other soldiers, and scan for the location of the incoming fire. He knew that being there mattered.

Just then, he heard "Striker Four Five, Striker Four Five."

He jumped back on the radio and leaned in the driver's side as far as he could to see the progress of the medic. The gunner's brain matter oozed from the top of his forehead where the round had entered. His eyes were open but glazed over. It was at that moment the medic lifted his eyes to meet Cory's. Knowing what he needed to hear, Cory made eye contact with him.

"Let him go," Cory said.

It was a confusing and devastating command for the medic who was also operating a vehicle and one of only three men defending their position–and Cory knew that.

Death wasn't like the movies where the fallen soldier took a few neat breaths and finally expired. No. The Iraqi soldier was gone. Gone but not gone. The decisions were hard: save but can't; treat but do no more harm. It was over somehow. Just over.

Cory told him things like, "It wasn't your fault," and "We told them to get out of there." And, he knew in the long run, the medic wouldn't be consoled.

Three Quick Reactionary Force trucks suddenly pulled up. As though they were meandering to a firing range for some refresher training, the base commander and his men got out of their vehicles.

Cory, somewhat amused, met the commander at the back of the vehicle while trying to mirror the commander's casual attitude. He should have at least crouched, but somehow, he felt embarrassed not to show the same amount of uninformed bravery as the QRF. In the background, the machine gun fire went "Ta-ta-ta-ta-ta...baa-baa-baa-baa."

"So, what's the situation?" the commander asked loudly.

As Cory heard bullets snap and zing nearby, sending puffs of dirt in their direction, he replied, "Sir, you are currently under fire from–" he pointed at multiple desert directions and at the puffs of dirt.

Once the point was made, Cory asked that they seek cover behind his vehicle. Since the commander now knew the situation, Cory waited for the commander to take over the operation. In Cory's mind, that made perfect sense. After all, the Infantry battalion commander who was more than experienced, competent, and a great leader, outranked Cory.

But to his surprise, the only thing he heard come out of the commander's mouth was, "Where do you need us?"

Evidently, Cory was trusted and still in charge. Amazed and

amused, but with no time to reflect on it, he requested the QRF go to the extreme right flank which was where Cory needed a vehicle that he could communicate with.

All the chaos, jammed communications, and many moving parts to the adrenalin fueled combat situation made repositioning entire U.S. formations of personnel and equipment impossible–pretty much the normal leadership challenge when under attack.

With all the air-support temporarily off-station, Cory wanted to move each vehicle, in intervals, with radio coordination, through the entire suspected battlefield. Without being able to physically see every enemy position, the only way to find and neutralize them was to move forward and fight through them.

He hoped that all the RPG danger had passed–it had been almost fifty minutes. Besides, any additional RPGs might just be taped, or safety pinned again, which meant the men firing them apparently didn't know enough to remove the tape so they'd explode on impact. Regardless once the commander was in position, everything went into motion. Cory moved his Humvee about twenty meters and then signaled for the QRF to do the same. He repeated the steps on his left and right, back and forth.

The other vehicles followed suit. Turret gunners fired, clearing hills and ridge tops to their immediate fronts. The QRF ran into the concentrated portion of the enemy that Cory anticipated on his right side. A heavy volume of automatic machinegun fire riddled an obscured portion of ridge. He continued the orders.

Radio communications were sporadic, with bits and pieces of information breaking through. Cory could picture what had unfolded and was ready to advance the rest of the vehicles through. For another kilometer they leapfrogged across the ridged terrain. Cory turned the entire formation, wheeling it right.

A few mud and mortar-structured villages needed to be cleared in the distance. The commander would take the first village closest to the right and Cory, with the other trucks, would race across the now flat and dusty desert to the second.

It was incredible to see several combat vehicles online, abreast, both left and right, sending dust skyward across the desert floor, rapidly closing the distance on the villages.

Cory saw the right flank vehicles reach their village. All the trucks and Humvees were online like a Patton tank charge making its way side by side past the commander's village position. It was a perfect moment. A photographic moment. One that Cory certainly appreciated.

Making a quick turn around after making a sweep of the small village, Cory heard that there was a situation and he was needed at the QRF's new position. There are often instances in combat where there is not enough information to make an informed decision. To Cory, considering the events of the day so far, that radio call could have meant anything. The tone in the voice, however, hinted that help was needed, so he double-timed to that position.

In the QRF village, soldiers and Iraqi police forces were running around and maneuvering their trucks. The commander was standing in the center of all the necessary chaos waiting for him.

As Cory got out and approached the commander, an enemy KIA was laying nearby. The commander looked a bit disappointed. All Cory could think to say was something that might help explain to a conventional Army commander the brand of Iraqi soldier that Ali and his men were.

"Sir," he started, indicating with a nod of his head toward Ali's forces. "They sometimes do things their own way here, but we need to continue to advise them. This is as much a psychological campaign as it is a military one. They are a force that is sending a message to the enemy out here in the Al Jazeera. They are the ones who strike fear into the enemy–not us."

The commander shook his head. "Are we done here?"

Cory indicated that the QRF could report back to base and thanked them for coming to their aid.

Returning to his Humvee, Cory watched through the windshield. While not exactly a textbook-perfect battle response for his team that day, Ali and his unit's fierce reputation would precede them from this day forward. The entirety of Al Jazeera would hear about Ali and his men. And in the cities, the story and fear would travel even faster.

Those Iraqi reputations contributed heavily to Cory's and his team's protection against future attacks, IEDs, snipers, or other ambushes. They were safe as long as they had units like Ali's along with the team.

Alone, the allied units would be at the *mercy* of units like Ali's. A tenuous balance at best.

CHAPTER THIRTY-THREE

Later in the day, various elements reported their status and location by radio. Back at the ambush sight Cory watched all the military elements loitering about creating a circus-like atmosphere.

Iraqis danced traditional dances with their arms linked to form a circle. They sang an Arabic song which they all seemed to know.

It looked like a parking lot of disorder with blue and white pickup trucks, tan Humvees, large cargo vehicles and the even-larger combat types.

Besides those walking and zigzagging about, other people stood in small groups, hands animating their stories while weapons hung from their shoulders. Captured suspected enemy personnel were being gathered for transportation and further questioning.

Assembled around another white pickup truck several more Iraqis played and took pictures. Six mangled bodies were in the bed of the truck, stacked like floppy rag dolls, all in civilian clothing. The shredded clothing hung off them like a horrific

Halloween costume.

Blood swished side to side in the bed of the truck, flies stuck in the long, already-matted and bloody hair. Jagged bullet holes had caused compound fractures and shattered faces. The head of one combatant with long purple hair was half blown away.

As the Iraqis tried to sit the body up for evidentiary photographs, the brains began to slide out and over the edge of his skull. Quickly, like catching something before it hits the ground, an Iraqi caught them and tried to put them back into the skull, but it looked like spaghetti dangling down the side of a dented pot.

Once he was in the sitting position, if the damaged side was turned away, the viewer saw a normal face. But once he was repositioned, Cory could see him clearly and his mind struggled to compute what he observed. While it all seemed surreal in a way, Cory also understood the impact and importance of the photos and the psychological warfare they represented.

While he understood, he couldn't remain and watch. He walked away before the rest of the bodies were photographed for the reports. For the first time that day he surveyed the battlefield in its entirety. He saw it all much clearer than ever before. He looked to his right and remembered the wadi and beyond where the flashes had come from and then looked to the right front where his Iraqi counterpart stood defiantly.

He looked a little further left where the helo had sent hellfire and mini gun fire onto the enemy positions that had kept the team pinned down. Then he looked straight ahead and watched in his mind's eye the RPGs come bouncing right in front of him.

Further to his left he remembered the accurately placed shots that impacted, spidering out on the bulletproof glass. As Cory walked away, the Explosives Ordinance Division (EOD) soldier called out to him after he passed the bridge.

"Hey. Just thought you'd want to know. Got a misfire. We found explosives set under the bridge. The blasting caps detonated but they must have been jerked out of the main charge . . . and we found a few RPG rounds up there and they didn't–"

Cory cut the investigator off. "I know–they had tape and safety pins still in them, right?"

Too weary to continue the conversation, Cory just waved an acknowledgement for the EOD's efforts, then took one last look at all the revelry and walked back to his vehicle. He had seen it all that day. The attack had every deadly element an ambush could consist of–to include a booby-trapped bridge full of explosives.

He then heard the muffled, scratchy radio call out one last time, "Striker Four Five, can we get a sitrep?"

* * *

In his study Cory notes his comfortable surroundings which contrast so much with the life he once lived. He walks to the desk and picks up a copy of the *American Legion* magazine, a gift subscription from someone he doesn't know.

It had started arriving in his mailbox about three months after he'd retired. He has no idea who paid for it, but it is always renewed. His calls to the publisher have only revealed that it is a gift subscription.

And then there was the beautiful thank you letter he'd received in 2012 for placing flags at the National Cemetery, only he'd never done such a noble thing.

And now the call about the script. The script he hadn't mailed out since 1994. The one he's just discovered isn't in the bottom drawer of his desk where he stored it.

When alone, he misses the noise of Army life. It's difficult no longer belonging to something bigger than himself. He slowly moves on to doing other things, though. It just takes time to adjust to life as a civilian, he thinks, often. Every now and then he still wonders about his Special Forces friends. Cory always hoped they were well and finally at peace.

Maybe he is, too. He hopes that for himself, despite the losses he's experienced. It's an odd, mixed feeling–to enjoy peace when so many others never got a chance at it. He shakes his head.

In 2004, the traumatic brain injury and partial paralysis served as the catalyst for the end of his military career. But before full retirement came, he chose to stay in and fight the war instead of accepting an early medical retirement. Cory continued to serve as best he could for as long as he was able. And if he could, he would run up that hill and courageously "take that seat" all over again.

His last combat deployment ended in December 2010. Over his career, he was deployed eighteen times to the Middle East, East Africa, and Southwest Asia, and he was medically retired in 2013 with a total of twenty-nine years of military service.

He was active duty for twenty-three years, of which eighteen years were spent in Special Forces; fourteen of those on a Special Forces Operational Detachment–Alpha (ODA). Additionally, Cory served three years as a Special Forces Underwater Operations (SFUWO) Instructor at the elite Combat Diver School.

On his wall, there is a plaque with the phrase: "You know that bad feeling? Get used to it, boys, because it's the way of life for the Combat Diver."

Reflecting on those days, Cory knows they'd all thrived on the risk and danger. The adrenalin, the knowledge that they would do what most could not; it was just the way they were designed to serve. A special breed; one that didn't fit in anywhere else.

He prays that he's made a difference. He drops the magazine back on the desk.

Obviously, someone seems to think that he did.

CHAPTER THIRTY-FOUR

Cory makes his way to Hollywood from his nearby home in San Jose and to the office of the executive who is sitting across from him on the other side of the desk. The executive is flipping through the screenplay as he looks at Cory.

"I can see why you would want to write, 'Where the Heart Lies.' It must have been hard dealing with all those memories of your time in Iraq."

"That's not why I wrote the story," Cory replies. "They weren't memories when I wrote it. The story wrote *me*." He looks around the room, then back at the executive. "I didn't have much choice," he finishes with a half-smile on his lips.

The executive pauses a moment. "What do you mean?"

"I finished writing the screenplay in 1994, a decade *before* I ever saw Iraq."

The exec's brows go up. "1994! But how? What could have inspired you to write–your future? I'm confused. I don't quite understand."

"I'm not sure I understand it myself, at least not in any way that I can fully explain. But, I'm at peace with it now. How could

I have known the future and write such a similar account? I didn't know the future." He shrugs. "I admit, it does seem coincidental. But after wrestling with this for a while, I've come to understand something. I wrote about who I always *wanted* to be. And if you want something bad enough, you will live that life. In the story, I'm all those guys.

"I'm the unsure Al, the dopy-looking Billy, and I am my own hero. That's why I wanted to go back to Iraq over and over. I had to see how the story would end. Does the hero have a life of courage, bravery, honor, and continue to win respect? Or does he lose that courage, cave to the fear, and lose the respect of those around him? Once again, I am all the characters in my story. Hero and sometimes not the hero. Isn't that who we *all* are, though?" Again, he shrugs. "It's okay. I began living my life story by knowing who I ultimately would become. I only wish I could have helped my dad more before he died like he did."

"Why did you wait so long to send this story out?" the executive asks, his hands now resting quietly on the desk.

Cory smiles and shakes his head. "I didn't send it out–at least not after 1994."

"Well, maybe your family sent it, then?"

"No sir. I checked with my sister and she's all the family I have. I can't explain how you got this unless you've had it since 1994."

The executive looks at Cory a long time, then nods, ever so slightly. He gets to his feet and offers Cory his hand.

"I can assure you that it arrived to me much more recently than that. I really, really like this script and I knew there was more to the story. Evidently, I need to thank your secret admirer for sending it to me. And I will fight to sell it to the agency. Unfortunately, right now they think a woman going through

Navy Seal training might be a better story. For what it's worth, I think they're wrong. I hope someone does make this film. Thank you for coming out to meet with me. I had to speak with you personally–your script has inspired me since I read it. And, for what it's worth, I think you did more for your dad than you will ever realize."

Cory shakes his hand, accepts the tattered manila envelope and tucks it under his arm. He turns to leave the office, but he's stopped momentarily.

"I'm curious," the executive says. "If you wrote this before you realized it was about who you wanted to be, why did you name your character Cory?"

Cory smiles and waves his hand. "I don't know. I just always knew that was his name, too. Like I said, I guess it chose *me* a long time ago."

EPILOGUE

After his visit with the Hollywood executive, Cory went home and turned his story into a book that included his real-life accounts–just like this one. He then faded into the ranks of all the quiet veterans who have stories to tell and lessons they hope to pass along. For him, that journey was complete, and that long chapter of his life was finally closed.

He enjoys holidays and adventures, serving others and doing good. And when he's home alone, he often reflects about his service to his country and friends.

The American Legion Magazine comes as a gift and he takes care to read it; after all, someone thinks enough of him to send it. Maybe someday he'll find out who ….

* * *

Many, many years later, on a quiet street outside the Detroit city limits, where the manicured lawns and sidewalks are shaded with mature sycamore trees, an old Victorian house sits with a flag swaying in the wind.

The mailman walks along, stops at the mailbox, deposits a single envelope, and continues whistling along his way.

With every shade drawn, most of the mid-morning sun is kept out. Old furniture and appliances fill the home. A grandfather clock stands tall and ominous, clicking slowly and rhythmically next to a steep staircase. Although the long-necked hammer never stops rocking, the hands ceased to move long ago; symbolic of a home, a time and place, that never moves forward.

Down a darkened hallway in a small room, a slow-turning fan slaps its edges harmlessly against a wind-carried drapery panel. Beyond the room, at the end of the hallway is a much larger room. A faded Persian rug covers the floor, and a large dark leather chair occupies its center. Seen from behind, thick clouds of whirling smoke gently rise to the ceiling. Beyond the chair is an old film showing on the plaster wall. A gray projector clicks loudly as it rotates the reels. The film slacks and catches every other turn. Dust particles dance in the light.

In the chair, sits a man consumed by what he sees. Almost bald, except for some lengthy white strands of hair, his bony hand slowly repositions the smoldering pipe in his mouth.

Behind him, a tattered sheaf of papers sits on a shelf. The movie script is reflected in the mirror. Along the spine, written in black marker it reads, "Where the Heart Lies." Also reflected backwards is the author's name which reads, "yroC." The framed picture of a proud and confident Green Beret sits on the shelf as well.

The man is sitting, watching a black and white military film reel. He is an old man now with a beautiful secret. He sits in the parlor and puffs on his pipe reminiscing of better times. He hardly understands that he is now a hero he never intended to be.

He sacrificed, not counting it sacrifice, in order that someone else might live better. It had saddened him to learn the homeless man had done the very thing he himself had contemplated. Yet in some ways that man who stepped onto the tracks to end his life, unintentionally helped someone else. Several others, it would turn out.

Disappearing into the shadows that day, hoping he made a difference too, the old man with tears in his eyes turns and looks at the photo of the Green Beret.

"I love you, Son."

* * *

Down at the mailbox, the door falls back open. In it is a renewal offer for another year's subscription and is addressed to: Robert McGuire, 5315 Ellis Street, Detroit, Michigan.

AUTHOR THOUGHTS

Never be afraid to invest yourself in others. It is risky, and I get it. If we lose them, it hurts. But sometimes hurting is okay. It is better to experience the loss of a friend or loved one, than to die having never truly known anyone – or they you. We are not much good to a world full of loss, if we always live our lives avoiding pain. Blessed are those who mourn, for they will be comforted. Blessed are the merciful, for they will be shown mercy. So, we might say, blessed are those who care.

Don

ABOUT THE AUTHOR

 Don Kabrich was born in Northern California in 1965. He is a husband, father, pastor, and veteran of the US Army Special Forces.

He first joined the military in 1983 and retired in 2013 at Fort Campbell, Kentucky. His awards include the Bronze Star medal, Purple Heart, and sixteen other military ribbons.

He earned his bachelor's degree from San Jose State University in behavioral science and his graduate degree from Gordon Conwell Theological Seminary in theology and biblical studies. He is currently pursuing a doctoral degree in pastoral theology. Don is a Boston Marathon finisher and a Mount Everest Base Camp trekking enthusiast. He currently serves as a minister to senior adults.

Don is a speaker and writer, seeking to encourage everyone placed in his path. His website is www.DonKabrich.com. If you'd like to contact him, he can be reached via email at donkab1@yahoo.com.